JAN SHIRLEY

rbP

Ragged Bears Publishing

RAGGED BEARS
Published by Ragged Bears Publishing Ltd.
Unit 14A, Bennetts Field Industrial Estate,
Southgate Road,
Wincanton,
Somerset BA9 9DT, UK

First published 2011
1 3 5 7 9 10 8 6 4 2

ISBN 978 1 85714 450 5
Printed in Poland

Jan Shirley writes ...

Dangerous, tricky, beautiful things, words, I love them. The same goes for people, really. Writing this story has meant I could play to my heart's content with both at once. What gets me going is the way we all manage to misunderstand each other, be so sure we're right and 'they' are wrong – look at young Krenn, dear little prig that she is – and yet we don't usually mean any harm. My story is fiction, but the archaeological details have been carefully researched and checked.

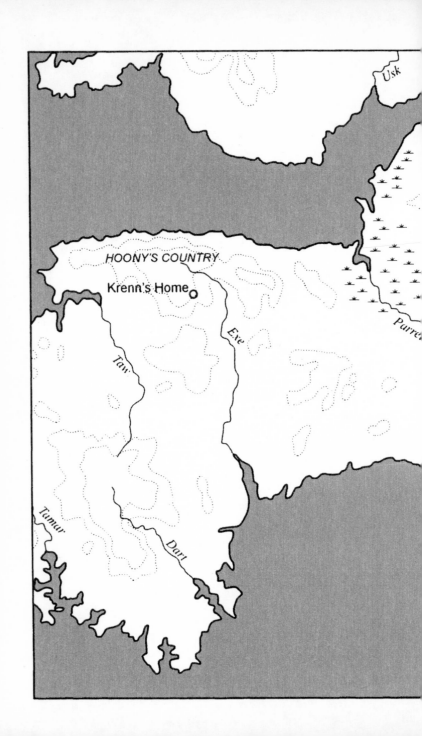

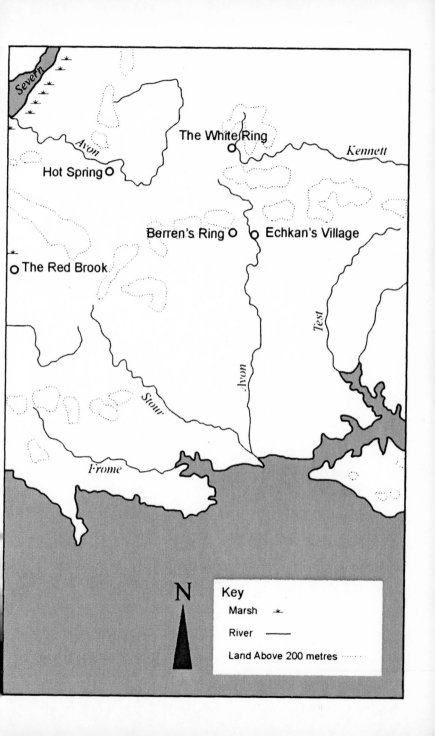

CHAPTER ONE
Outsider

'We owe her nothing. Seven years' care, eight, she owes us. She ought to go away from us as naked as we found her!' It was Ensy speaking, Old Woman of the tribe, priestess. 'But of course we shan't do that. I've given her warm clothing, and food for six days. It's all we can spare.'

'She can travel with us to begin with, surely,' said Hoony. He had obeyed his own mother when she was Old Woman and he was going to obey Ensy, but it wouldn't be easy. He could remember her as a bossy little girl and then as a nagging wife – one of Haldo's thanks be! not his – and he wished very much that the Stone hadn't had to go to her. 'She can travel with us to begin with,' he repeated.

'No. We are to go south, the Old Woman said so, and Krenn is to go and find this temple of hers. There's nothing like that to the south of us, she'll have to go east. That's where the great temples are.'

7

Hoony and his people were busy packing up for the move. There was no time to lose, it was already well into autumn and the seed should have been in the ground by now. Most of them would much rather have stayed where they were and got on with the planting and risked a bad winter and worn-out soil, but the goddess had to be right. If She says go, you go.

But they would have to hurry. Even if they only went down river along the Barle to the land they'd left a dozen years ago – it should have recovered by now – it would take them several days. Goats can be made to move quite fast, cows are not too bad, but pigs are the most contrary beasts the Lady ever made. Then when they arrived and had put up houses and a fence to keep the stock in and the wolves out, they must start the autumn slaughtering and preserving, not to mention clearing the ground and getting next year's crops planted. What they'd have to do now was send an advance party to start putting up shelters. Was it worth taking the roof-trees with them, or should they cut fresh when they got there? Hoony had a thousand and one things on his mind; he hadn't the time to quarrel with Ensy over Krenn. Besides, Ensy spoke for the Lady, and that was that.

'Krenn, Krenn, where are you?' he called. 'Ah, there you are. Ens – the Old Woman's right, you go east. Flint-traders and other people, they come from that way, and I've heard some of them talking about the great temples they have over there. Much bigger than any of ours, so they say. But they're a long way off, you'll have to keep on and on. Keep going towards the sun as it rises, and the holy Mother go with you.' He slung a short deerskin cloak off his shoulders and put it round hers. 'My mother dressed these skins for me – wear it for me and for her.' He kissed her, and turned away to get on with taking down the roof-trees.

Ensy flushed an angry red and began to mutter something about wicked wastefulness but Hoony stared her down and she was quiet.

Young Jinsy came rushing up. He had loved Krenn all his life and he was furious.

'I'm going with her!' he shouted. 'You're wicked, wicked and cruel! How can you send her out all alone like that, when she's lived with us ever since she was born?'

Krenn herself looked at him in horror. That anyone should speak like that about an order of the Old Woman, of the goddess! She wouldn't have been surprised to see him struck by lightning.

What did strike him, and hard, was his mother's fist. Delighted to be able to relieve her feelings and do right at the same time, Ensy dealt him a hearty clip on the side of the head and knocked him flying. No one took very much notice. Krenn looked to where he curled up in the lee of one of the houses, rubbing his head – yes, he was all right. She nodded goodbye to all her non-relatives, picked up her bundle and went away.

All this happened because once upon a time, around five thousand years ago, a tiny new-born baby girl had been found in thick woodland, found and rescued. Now she was seven, going on eight.

'Tell me again, Nanna,' she would say to the old woman who loved her, 'tell me about when I was found in the forest.' And the old woman would tell her all over again about the time Hoony's people were travelling through the forest and how one day they came to a place where other people had camped before them and they thought they could hear a child crying.

'And that was me, Nanna, that was me!'

'Yes, that was you. They'd put you out to die, but you'd been well wrapped up in a fine piece of stuff, not leather, very soft, it was like nothing we'd ever seen – someone loved you all right, and there you were alive and yelling. You weren't going to die, not you! And the men said, "Don't look for it, leave it, it can't be healthy, wouldn't have been put out if it was all right," but my own daughter's baby had just died, she still had the milk in her breasts and it was hurting her because there wasn't any baby to take it away. So she said, "Find it, find it, give it to me!" and I looked among the trees and under the bushes and there you were, bawling with rage! And I unwrapped you and looked at you and you were a fine girl child, no mark or damage of any kind, and I gave you to my own girl to suckle. How she cried out with relief as you began to take the milk from her, poor girl!'

'Had I been there long, Nanna? Why didn't a wolf take me? Or a bear?'

'Long enough! We found the ashes of their fire, those strangers, whoever they were, and they were three or four days old. And the wolves and the bears – well, either they weren't feeling very hungry, or the Great Mother protected you! I was quite sure She'd saved you to be a blessing to my own girl, and so I wouldn't let the men kill you or leave you behind. I'm the one who says who lives and who dies in this family, they know that!'

'Well yes, I should think so,' said Krenn. Hoony was Old Man of the family but it was the women, especially the Old Woman, Hoony's mother, who mattered. They made all the decisions. When it was time for the family to shift to a new district, which of the newborn babies were to be kept and which put out to die, which sick people would get better and ought to be helped and which ones put out in the woods to go to the goddess – all that sort of thing.

'I should think so! But then she went and died herself.'

'Not for a long time,' said the Old Woman, smiling at Krenn, 'not till after your naming. You remember her, don't you?'

'Of course I do, very well. I loved her a lot. But, Nanna, I wish you hadn't let them call me Krenn, 'doesn't belong', I don't like it. Why did you?'

'Because it was true. You don't belong to our family, or to any of the families that use the forest. They were strangers passing through, those people who left you, they were *krenn*. Even the stuff you were wrapped in, we've never used anything like that, never seen such a thing. It's no use pretending.'

'Three whole years,' said Krenn, 'you'd think they'd have forgotten I was *krenn* by that time.'

Children in this family were not given names until they had stayed alive for at least three years and you could be fairly sure you were not going to lose them. The names all had meanings – Hoony was 'strong right hand', young Jinsy was 'jumps first, thinks later', Krenn was 'not one of ours'. 'Nanna' was only a nickname – the true name of the Old Woman, like the Name of the goddess, the Great Mother, the Lady, was never spoken.

Krenn was almost eight now, and a useful member of the family, even if she didn't belong to it. She was quick, clever, patient. Like all her friends, she would far rather herd pigs or round up goats or go hunting for wild foods and medicine plants than do boring jobs like grind corn, but she knew they none of them had any choice. And you could talk and sing, and take turns at the grinding; it wasn't too bad.

Her friends didn't often call her Krenn, they called her Sparrow. Small, quickmoving and brown haired, she did sometimes look rather like one. But they always remembered that she didn't belong. One day one of the older girls, Kallo, happened to say, 'It'll be sad for you, Krenn, when we're grown up. You'll be all alone and miserable when we're with our men and having babies.'

'Why?' said Krenn in surprise. 'I'm perfectly all right, I shall have very good babies.'

'Not if no one wants you. And they won't, not with you being *krenn*. Who'd want a *krenn* mother for his children?' 'It's not her fault,' put in soft-hearted Sooral, and smiled at Krenn.

Krenn turned and ran to ask the Old Woman about this. Then as she came near her house, she heard her singing, and stopped outside. The Old Woman was singing to the family's most treasured possession, the sacred Stone. Krenn dropped down onto the ground and waited. She couldn't go in, no one did; the Stone was very holy, and no one must ever see it except the Old Woman herself, or only when something hugely special was happening. Normally it stayed high up on a shelf, wrapped carefully in a piece of deerskin, but sometimes it had to be taken out, polished, sung to, shown respect. Endless long years ago, the Goddess herself had given it to the first Old Woman of the family, and she had given it to the next, and so on and so on for ever and ever since the world began. It was dark, heavy, a little blackish lump of shiny stone no bigger than Krenn's two fists held close together, and on one side of it was a brilliant patch of white, quite small, shaped rather like a leaf, or like the moon when it's almost full.

Krenn listened, and sang the holy tune along in her mind as her Nanna's voice went on. The singing was soft and shaky, for the Old Woman was very, very old. Krenn shivered, as it crossed her mind for the first time that one day her Nanna would die, and what would become of her then?

Was it true, would no one want her? Would she have to go out into the forest and manage on her own? But no one could possibly do that. You die in the forest if you're all alone, everyone knew that. It didn't seem worth having been saved all those years ago if she was going to be turned out now for the wolves and the bears.

Then the singing stopped and the Old Woman called, 'Krenn? Come in.'

Krenn put the door-curtain aside but didn't go in. This was her own home, but she kept out of it when the Stone was uncovered. Had the Old Woman put it away? Yes, it was safe, she could go in.

'There you are, child!' said the old lady, frowning. 'I've got things to say to you – it's like this, Sparrow. I'm anxious, very anxious. We should have left this place weeks ago. A year ago, really, but there it is, we didn't. Weeks ago, certainly. The ground is used up, finished, no good any more, and we ought to have gone. We ought to be finding a new place and getting settled in before the winter comes.'

'But this is a good place, Nanna. We've always had good crops here – well, always until this year, I suppose.'

'That's it, this year. The goodness is worn out, finished, we should have gone.'

Krenn waited, not liking to ask why they hadn't. There was a long silence. Krenn's knee itched, but she kept still.

'If the winter's late,' said the Old Woman, 'if only the winter's late, then we still have time. Sparrow, do you know why we didn't go?'

Krenn shook her head. Of course she didn't.

'Because of you.'

'Me? Oh Nanna, when did I ever get to decide anything?'

'Be quiet, girl! Yes, because of you. I am very old, too old. Useless. Next time the family moves, they will leave me behind.'

'Oh no!' Then Krenn saw – yes, of course, if you were very old and no use, not worth your food, you were sent out into the woods and you went to the goddess. 'But Nanna, you've got the Stone, you have to take care of that, they can't send you to Her!'

'Oh can't they?' The Old Woman smiled grimly. 'There's always another ready and waiting. Ensy will be Old Woman after me.'

'Ensy! But you hate her!'

'No. We don't often agree, but that's different. Inside the family, hatred is dangerous, not allowed. Love your own, hate outsiders, that's the rule. You know that very well.'

'Don't I just! All right, you don't hate Ensy. But she hates me, Nanna, you know she does. Has it got to be her?'

'Certainly. She's my grandmother's great-great-grandchild.'

'Will she have the Stone?'

'Of course.'

'What will she do about me?'

Krenn could almost have thought the Old Woman was crying. She put her arms round the girl who was no relation to her and rocked to and fro, yes, weeping.

'I've done wrong, Sparrow, very wrong. I've let myself love you, and you're none of mine, you're *krenn*, and I've put the family in danger for your sake. Wrong, wrong!'

'Nanna, I don't understand.'

'Of course you don't.' The old lady pulled herself together and stopped crying. 'It's like this, we ought to have moved on by now, found new ground, I should have given the order, and I've kept putting it off. I didn't do it –'

'Because you'd have had to be left behind and die?'

Krenn got an irritated shake. 'No! Because you would! They'd have left me and they'd have left you. You're nearly eight, aren't you? Well, that's eight years Ensy has been resenting you, she thinks I did wrong to bring you into the family, and so I did, so I did! "Love your own", I know the rule well enough, and you're not my own, nothing to do with me. But my girl loved you, Sparrow, and I love you, *krenn* or no *krenn*. But who else does? Once I'm dead, and I ought to be dead already, you won't have any friends.'

None, thought Krenn, none? What about Jinsy and Kallo, kind Sooral and Sarren and the others?

'I've held onto my life,' went on the Old Woman, 'when I should have let it go, I've put the family in danger from worn-out ground and a bad harvest, and all so as to keep you alive a little longer! What a fool I've been! I should have trusted the Lady!

And now – now I don't know whether Ensy will put you out in the forest or just not give you any food, but it won't make much difference.' The Old Woman shook her head sadly, still full of self-reproach. 'This year's harvest was bad and next year's will be worse if we use this soil again. Some of us will die of hunger and it will be my fault. Mine, and I'm the mother of the family, their guardian under Her! I have done very wrong.'

'Nanna, can't the Stone help? Won't it tell us what to do?'

'How often have I got to tell you that the Stone doesn't tell us things? It's a precious tool given us by the Mother, it's sacred, it's holy, but it is not a god!'

'Yes, Nanna, I remember, I'm sorry.'

'But yes, I have asked the Stone. That's to say, I have asked the goddess through the Stone, and now I see my way clear. She has told me, She has shown me the right path.' The old lady smiled happily and tightened her arm round Krenn. 'I have confessed my sin to Her and She forgives me, and now – listen, Sparrow! – now I see that although I have no business to love you, because you aren't mine, She has! She can, She does, because everything belongs to Her, She made it all. I can quite safely give you to Her, because you are hers already. Sun, moon and stars, forest, rivers and sea, She made them all. All their spirits obey Her, trees or streams or animals, birds, all things come from Her and all return to Her!'

Krenn didn't like the sound of that one little bit. All sorts of things were regularly given to the goddess, she knew that – grain, baked cakes, blood from animals they'd killed – but people? People? Krenn passionately hoped not.

'It is laid on me,' went on the Old Woman cheerfully, 'that the family must move, now, now at once while the new moon is waxing. There's still time if the cold and the rains are late, and they will be, I know that. I shall die and be buried, you will go to the goddess, and the family will move to new ground and grow good food.' She fell silent, gazing happily into the distance.

'Nanna, if I've got to go to the Lady – Nanna, how?'

'Eh? Didn't I say? I must be getting old! On your feet, Sparrow, on your own two feet, walking. I saw you clearly, She showed me and I saw you, walking among huge tall stones. You were inside a Circle, not one of ours, bigger, much bigger, enormous, a long way away and very holy. I saw you walk across it and kneel down and make an offering – what it was, I couldn't see. But there you were, and I knew as clearly as I've ever known anything in all my born days that you are to go and find this temple, and there find your own people. Your own people, and you won't be *krenn* any longer, you'll be beloved, precious, Andal. Everything will be all right.' She beamed at the bewildered girl and added, 'Go and find that Ensy for me, my darling, tell her I want her.'

Shaking her head to try to clear it, Krenn went. What large ideas her Nanna had! And however was she supposed to find a strange and holy temple somewhere a long way away? She would be dead of cold and hunger, if not wild beasts, inside three days. In the forest, you die.

'Crazy!' said a low voice close to Krenn as she sat in the firelight after the evening meal. 'Stark staring raving crazy! Don't you pay any attention to her, Sparrow!'

'Jinsy! Oh how you made me jump. What do you know about it, anyway?'

'I listened outside the house. Saw you go in, thought I'd check. Listen, Sparrow, we ought to have moved, right, and if she wants to she can stay behind when we go and turn up her toes, fine, no one'll stop her, but to send you out like that, no! She's gone right out of her tiny little mind.'

'Jinsy, you're only a boy, you don't understand. She's the Old Woman, for goodness' sake! You shouldn't even have gone near her house.'

'Good thing I did,' said Jinsy. 'I'm going to tell Hoony, and he'll –'

'No, you mustn't, he can't! Only women talk to the Great Mother, not men, you know that. Do talk sense, Jinsy!'

'All the same, I –'

'Ssh! Look!'

The Old Woman hadn't eaten with the family that night, but that needn't have meant anything; she often ate alone in her own house. She was the Lady's servant, after all. But now the curtain across her doorway was flung back and she came out, leaning on Ensy's arm. Ensy was tall and strong and had a lot of teeth. Her name meant 'strong minded'. She had three daughters and five sons all alive, a record none of the other mothers in the family could match. Sooral was her eldest child, and Jinsy, born a few days after Krenn had been found, was the youngest of the sons.

'What's Mother –?'

'Ssh!'

The Old Woman and the younger one came into the circle of firelight and stood still. The Old Woman shook off the support of Ensy's hand and moved forward. Ensy waited in the background, looking smug.

'The family is to move to a new home. It will move at once, tomorrow, and go south till it finds good ground. The moon is still new, increasing, blessed be She! Now is the time to go. You will leave me behind. You will leave Krenn behind too. Ensy will explain, she knows. Ensy will be Old Woman after me, and her own name will never be spoken again. Now I give her the sacred Stone of our people, and my blessing. May the holy Mother guide and keep her!' Krenn watched as her Nanna took the wrappings off something she had in her hands and held it up high so that they could all see it. It was the Stone, small, dark and glinting in the firelight. People who happened to be standing dropped quickly to their knees, men covered their eyes. Ensy put out her hands to receive the Stone, took it, wrapped it quickly and held it close. Then she turned round and vanished into the house that till now had belonged to Krenn's Nanna.

The nameless old woman stood alone near the flickering fire, trembling. She put out a hand and said, 'Sparrow, where are you?' Krenn was already halfway across the clearing and was just in time to put her arm round her foster-grandmother before she gave two or three violent shivers and fell. Hoony ran forward to help her and between them they carried her into Hoony's house.

Nameless old woman, Hoony's mother, Krenn's beloved Nanna, she was not left in the forest to die of cold and hunger. She died peacefully that night in her son's arms, and knew what was happening.

'You see,' she whispered to Krenn, smiling, 'I'm allowed to die here with you and be buried. That shows my sin is forgiven and my sacrifice accepted.' Krenn smiled back through her tears and did not say, 'But who said you could sacrifice me?'

Next morning, Krenn and all Hoony's people threaded their way through the forest and climbed the hillside till they came to the ancient burial mound their family always used. There they stowed what was left of their Old Woman comfortably away in a corner of her own, ready for her life in the next world. She lay close to the remains of her many relatives, decently dressed in her best clothes, with her hair neatly fastened at the back of her head and held with a pair of bone pins. They used her best ones – Ensy said it was a waste, but Krenn put them in just the same and even Ensy left them as they were. They gave her the necessary food and drink, sang their farewells, closed the opening they'd made in the mound, and made the proper offerings to the Great Mother. Then the whole family, and Krenn, danced the death-dance in a long line, sun-wise, three times round the burial place, and came away.

If you are wondering where Krenn and Hoony's people were living, you get a clue just at the beginning of the next chapter where Krenn goes south from the place where the River Barle widens into swampy pools ringed with willows. This is now Withypool ('withy' means 'willow') on Exmoor.

CHAPTER TWO
Thief

So now here she was, all alone and heading east. Alone in the forest, you die, everyone knew that. But just for the moment Krenn was amazed to find that she liked being on her own. Was she creeping anxiously through the trees, looking out for dangers, jumping if a twig cracked? No, not a bit of it. She strode confidently along, Hoony's cloak swirling about her – it came almost to her feet – enjoying the sunshine that dappled down through the trees and stopping now and then to pick hazelnuts or a few late, flavourless blackberries. She kept mainly to the tops of the hills, where the going was easier.

She walked on with an odd feeling of holiday – no pigs to herd, no weeds to pull up, no squirrels to track down for their hoards of nuts, no skins to scrape and soften and work at, no pounding and pounding and pounding away at little gritty bits of corn that were never going to turn into flour – nothing to do except the absolutely impossible. Just find a great and holy temple far, far away in the east of the world and offer up an offering she hadn't got. Impossible, so why worry?

First, she thought, she would go to their own holy place. It's all your fault anyway, she would say to the Lady, you do something about it. Find my people for me. Please.

But if I found them, would I like them? They put me out to die.

But they had to. I suppose my mother had died, what else could they do? And they did wrap me up carefully, in my own good coverlet, I wasn't naked whatever Ensy says. Krenn smiled, and patted the bundle she was carrying. It had nuts and dried meat and griddle cakes in it and flints to make fire and a small flint knife, all wrapped together in the same piece of cloth, grey and brown with tan coloured stripes, that she'd been wrapped in herself when she was a yelling baby.

Krenn had been climbing fast, and now she stopped to draw breath. She was aiming for the holy circle that stood on the shoulder of a hill just south of the place where the River Barle widens into swampy pools ringed with willows.

She'd been there before, but not for some time, and never alone. The trees up here were mostly oak, with leaves on the point of falling. Krenn stood among them and looked – yes, there was the twisted tree, and then turn left. There were no paths to follow, but Krenn didn't need paths. Indeed, she thought they were dangerous – once get out onto a beaten open way like that and anything can jump you.

Then the trees thinned, and she knew she was coming to the circle. She stopped under the trees, not wanting to go out into the empty space. There was nothing growing inside the circle, nothing but grass and heather. From time to time the Old Woman would call some of the girls and women together and they would go and root out all the seedlings and young trees. It was an almost perfect round, about forty paces across, divided from the forest by a low earth bank, nothing else. An emptiness made for the goddess.

Krenn stood with her hand on the rough bark of a tree and looked at the hurdle filling in the entrance-gap. Under a tree, she felt safe, protected. Danger comes in the open. Then quickly she let go, walked forward, squeezed past the hurdle and was in the open round, no branches over her head, nothing between herself and her maker. But She can see me anywhere, Krenn reminded herself, and knelt down under the hot sun, who was the Lady's child. The blessed moon, she knew, would not rise till later in the day, almost evening, and was in her most fortunate and hopeful phase, a crescent just starting to grow larger. The best time to begin a journey.

She couldn't think of the right words, so just kept still and waited. A ladybird crawled up a blade of grass close by her right knee. Krenn watched it as it clung to the tip of the grassblade, trying to make up its mind whether to climb down again or fly away. Lady, she said in her mind, please look after me. Ladybird, ladybird, fly away home. Home, and where's that?

The grassblade bent and swung, the ladybird flew off. Krenn stood up, backed carefully out of the circle, walked all the way round outside it once, sunwise, and then turned east.

There were no sharp, jagged hills in Krenn's country, nothing but long rounded tops which seemed to go on for ever before they tumbled down at last in a steep, sudden slope. Down she would plunge into a valley, struggle through a tangle of trees and undergrowth and then have to climb just as steeply up again onto the next long hill. On and on she toiled, and began to feel tired. Depressed, too. Being all alone stopped being an amazing treat and was just miserably sad. And dangerous. She thought about Jinsy and her other friends, she even thought longingly of Ensy and her sharp voice telling you you'd missed half the weeds on the other side of the bean row. Dear Jinsy, just imagine him blazing out like that! She hoped Ensy hadn't hit him too hard.

Krenn was very hot. It was a warm autumn day and she had put on all the clothes she could find in case she needed them later, not to mention Hoony's cloak. Now she took this off and made it into a bundle round her package of food and flints. That was better. Six days' food, Ensy'd said. After that, how would she manage? She must keep a look out all the time for berries and nuts and anything else eatable. Fish, she'd be able to guddle fish, but she couldn't set snares, not when she had to keep travelling on. You have to leave snares and give the animals time to be caught, and she'd got to go and find this temple her Nanna had seen. She was just working out anxiously that she could probably manage to sleep safely if she climbed up each night into a good high tree, when she froze where she stood. Never mind about night dangers, there was something coming up the hill now.

Krenn scrambled quickly into the nearest tree. Was it wolves? Don't let it be a bear! Bears can climb. Holy Mother, I've only just started, give me a chance!

There was very little to hear, just an occasional crackle of twigs, a brushing of leaves. Deer wouldn't make even that much noise, but a wild boar – and then Krenn gave a sob of relief, dropped out of the tree and clutched Jinsy round the neck.

'Jinsy! Oh Jinsy, what's happened? Have they sent you to bring me back?'

'Ouf, Sparrow, no need to throttle me! Let go! And mind my arrows! You've made me drop everything.' He sat up and shook himself. 'I'm sorry, I'm sorry! But what is it? Have they changed their minds? And where are the others?'

'What others?' Jinsy was busy picking things up. 'There's no one here but me. I said I'd go with you, and I will. That's all.'

'Oh Jinsy! Then they don't – no, of course they don't. But they'd never let you, not in a thousand years!'

'They don't know anything about it. Far too busy packing up, all rushing round and tying themselves in knots. I just came away, Sparrow. Easy. Falling off a log.'

Krenn smiled at him lovingly and shook her head. Dear, daft, good silly Jinsy. Oh, how she did wish –

'Good, nice, darling Jinsy, now you've got to –'

'Not so much of the darling stuff, Sparrow. Whatever you're going to say – no.'

'Jinsy Old Woman's son, now you've got to go back.'

'No.'

'Back, you crazy fool.'

'No.'

'Back! I mean it. You've got a family, you've never been *krenn*, you don't know what it's like! Go on, go back quickly, they won't punish you too badly, not if you hurry.'

'And I thought you'd be glad to see me,' said Jinsy reproachfully.

'As if I'm not! Gladder than you can possibly imagine. All the same I'm not going to let you make yourself *krenn*. It's worse than you think. Come on now, little brother, turn round. Off you go.'

Jinsy smiled at her. He'd known she would do this, and he'd guarded against it. 'It's no good fussing, my old Sparrow. I can't go back. Can't, so there.'

'What do you mean, can't? Of course you can, and the sooner the better.'

'No. You'll understand why – but I'm not going to tell you yet, come on, let's get further away.' He glanced up at the sun, faced eastwards and set off.

There was nothing Krenn could do but follow him.

Hours later they stopped to rest. Jinsy drew a deep breath.

'Look, Sparrow, I've got to tell you. I'm beginning to wish I hadn't – well, I just did it, not sure how really, it seemed like a good – but never mind, look, I took this.'

He handed her a small wrapped bundle. Krenn took it, weighed it in her hands, and understood.

In absolute despair she sank down onto the forest floor. He had gone into the Old Woman's house, a place no man or boy could even enter, he had taken the Stone off its shelf and now he had brought it to her. He had stolen from the goddess.

If he took it back, they would kill him. Rightly.

Perhaps the Great Mother would kill him now anyway.

He had brought it to her so as to make sure she couldn't send him away. Couldn't send him back to face punishment. Made himself a thief, for her sake.

He had made her a thief too.

Did he expect her to be grateful?

Silent, furious, Krenn unfastened her own bundle, put the heavy little package into it and did it up again. Then she picked it up, settled it over her shoulder and set off again eastwards through the trees.

Neither of them spoke. They walked and walked, along flat hilltops, down into tangled river valleys, up again and on again, going all the time carefully, watchfully, looking out for dangers. But they met no bears, no wolves, nothing to alarm them.

At last the light began to fail.

'We'll have to stop before long,' said Jinsy, speaking for the first time since he had handed the Stone to Krenn, 'look out for a good tree to spend the night in.' He'd expected her to be angry, he'd known she would be furious, and yet he was desperately upset that she didn't seem to be glad he was there, didn't see what an appallingly dangerous thing he had done, stolen from the goddess, from the goddess! Just for her.

Couldn't she be just the smallest bit grateful?

'Yes,' said Krenn. 'And we'd better eat. Did you bring food?'

'No. But I can soon get some. Listen, there's water quite near.' He slipped ahead, then on and down a hillside. Krenn ran after him, and soon they came to a place where two rivers joined and the water spread out into pools and marshland. 'There'll be game here,' murmured Jinsy. 'Wait and be quiet.' He didn't need to tell her that.

Krenn knew how to hunt. She moved back out of the way, found a log and sat down. Through a tangle of branches she could just see the new moon, a slender crescent low down in the sky, and she prayed to it with all her heart.

Forgive us, forgive us and help us!

Jinsy got his bow off his back, strung it and fitted an arrow. Dusk already, dark soon – he stood heron still, waiting.

Duck flew over, but too far away. Three or four deer came nervously to drink, but were uneasy, restless, and vanished almost at once. Come on, thought Jinsy, come on, it's almost dark. Then there was a splashing and a rustling and a family of young pigs came down to the water's edge. Jinsy very slowly raised his bow, lined up on the nearest pig, and with the smallest movement of his fingers let go of the bowstring. The pig leapt, fell, thrashed screaming about in the water, and its brothers and sisters scattered and were gone. Jinsy and Krenn together fell on the wounded beast, grabbed it by the legs and ran with it up onto the bank. Jinsy had a knife ready, he quickly cut the pig's throat and it died.

They climbed up to a drier part of the wood, found kindling, struck flints and made a fire. Together they cut the pig up – it was a last year's one, the stripy markings on its fur long since gone, well-grown and with plenty of meat on it – and together they cooked it.

'Now will you say you're glad I came?' demanded Jinsy, as they sat warm and well fed by the glowing embers.

'Of course I am,' said Krenn. 'I hate you,' she added in a matter-of-fact voice, 'because you've made me worse than *krenn*, you've made me wicked, and I wasn't wicked before, but you're my own crazy Jinsy and if She kills us both, well then, She kills us.' With that, she fell fast asleep against his shoulder and he had to wake her up so that they could stow the cooked pigmeat safely in one good oak tree and get themselves into another.

'By the way,' said Krenn, as she began to doze off again, 'did you remember to get your arrow back?'

'Well, of course I did,' he answered. 'It's a good one, one of Shann's best, flint-tipped and all. I wasn't going to lose that.'

Krenn drew in her breath in a horrified laugh – 'Oh Jinsy, if the Mother doesn't get you, your big brother will! The quicker we go east, the better.'

Now Krenn and Jinsy struggle for several days and then at last get up onto what we call the Brendon Hills, and then the Quantocks. It was easier going on the hill tops, not so much undergrowth to get through. They had both lived among hills all their lives, which is why they get such a shock further on in Chapter Three.

CHAPTER THREE
World's End

Krenn woke often during the night. The crescent moon blazed among the stars. Krenn watched it and didn't know whether to feel reassured or terrified. Wherever you try to go, She has got there first.

Then while it was still dark but the birds were noisy and dawn was coming, she shook Jinsy, who woke at once. They climbed out of their tree, found the pigmeat still safe in the other, and got ready to go on with their journey.

'I don't think they'll have missed me yet,' said Jinsy. 'Hoony sent Ty and Sarrow off with an advance party yesterday and the rest aren't moving till first light today. With any luck both lots will think I'm with the other one.'

They set off through the trees, made a detour round the watersmeet, scrambled up and down hills, in and out of tangled valleys, till at last they got onto a long ridge that led in the right direction. The goddess might be hunting them, but for now the forest was quiet, and that was reassuring. They could hear nothing more than the normal dawn noises, birds wakening, animals going about their usual life.

On and on they went, east and east and east, through a scatter of pale birch trees, through oaks, through birches again. After a long time they sat down to rest and eat some of last night's cold roast pig.

'We need to keep a bit more north,' said Jinsy after a while. 'North and then east again. We must be just about south of the Long Road by my reckoning. That's the way the flint-sellers come, and everyone.'

'What everyone?'

'Oh, I don't know. Other people.'

'There aren't any other people, there's only us in the world.'

'Then where do the flint-men come from, and the men who trade axeheads? And you, Sparrow?'

'Yes, well, I suppose I know there must be other places and other people, I just can't imagine them, that's all.'

'Hoony's people and Dowan's people and

Jerro's people, and we all meet every year to worship the Great Mother and that's it?' said Jinsy, laughing at her. 'There's more to the world than that. All you girls think about is the ducks and the beans and the corn and the babies – we men get out into the world and see things and do things! We know what a big place it is, not just our little patch and our little bunch of families.'

'And a fine mess you'd be in if we didn't send you off out of our way!' retorted Krenn. 'All right, you go and enjoy yourselves and frighten all the game with your big talk, but you're glad enough to come home and eat the food we've been breaking our backs over, day after day!'

'Want any more?' asked Jinsy, pointing his fine flint knife at the pigmeat, and Krenn laughed and gave in. But she said no, she didn't want any more, it was time to get moving again, and they packed up and set off.

Krenn still had the holy and dangerous Stone wrapped up in her deerskin bundle. She had decided that all she could do was look after it the best she could and leave the rest to the goddess. If She had been going to strike them dead with a thunderbolt, wouldn't She have done it by now? Instead, She'd given them roast pig and a good night's sleep. As her Nanna used to say, who can understand the ways of the goddess? Get on with the next thing and leave the rest to Her.

The next thing at present was to find the Long Road. Krenn and Jinsy made a long loop northwards, keeping to the high ground round the heads of several difficult valleys, and at last came onto the east-west ridge Jinsy was looking for. It was a well-known route, but not a trodden road, scarcely even a path. They didn't expect to find it full of traders or hunting parties, but even so they approached it warily. For some moments they waited in the shelter of the trees, looking and listening. There was no one there. To the left the tree-cover thickened round the Long Road as it plunged down towards the river valley, to the right the hilltop highway led invitingly through open heathery patches and between clumps of tall limes, oaks and hollies.

'Lovely going,' said Jinsy. 'Get there in no time on this.'

'Get where?'

'Wherever we're going to.'

They walked, trotted, slept, ate, trotted, walked and went on walking. They walked right down off the Long Road ridge, across difficult low ground and then up again and onto another ridge, this one running south-east. They ate the remains of the pig, which lasted very well, and anything edible they could find growing. Once they saw travellers, six men with bundles slung on poles going westwards at a steady trot, but they hid till they'd gone by. The travellers' dogs scented Krenn and Jinsy and snuffled and barked a little, but they didn't insist on it and the trotting men took no notice.

Another time they saw a village down below them near a river and were strongly tempted to go and visit it, but in the end decided not to. They stood on the hillside above it, sniffing the smell of the fires, hearing the cows lowing and now and then a baby crying or someone shouting, and it sounded and smelt very homelike. But Jinsy shook his head.

'We need to go further than this,' he said.

'Much further,' Krenn agreed. They skirted carefully round, out of scent and hearing of the dogs.

At night they got themselves up above ground level again and slept safely though not comfortably high up in the trees, wedged into the crooks of branches. Once, before they'd eaten all the pigmeat, they were disturbed by a wild cat which came to the smell of the meat, but it hissed at them and vanished when they woke up and shouted at it. Twice they heard wolves calling to each other, and Krenn put out a hand to find Jinsy's and held it hard, but the sound never came close.

'Anyway,' said Jinsy, 'wolves aren't really dangerous. Shout loud enough, and they go away.'

Krenn smiled and said nothing.

They saw bear tracks once, quite fresh, but never saw or heard the bear.

Then suddenly one morning there were no more hills. They stood and looked out from the southern end of the ridge and there was nothing in front of them but flat marshland and bog. It spread out as far as they could see, a great dismal sheet of watery nothingness. Krenn was horrified.

'It's all wrong,' she said. 'All open. No trees, and no shape, nothing but flatness. If we go down there, we'll get lost, there's nothing to steer by.'

'Lost and then drowned,' agreed Jinsy. 'Still, there must be ways across it, there's nowhere else to go.'

'The proper world,' said Krenn angrily, 'has

hills in it. Hills and trees. How could the Mother have made a place like that? It's all wrong!'

'Perhaps it's just what was left over when She'd finished,' suggested Jinsy.

'It certainly looks like it. Have we got to get across this watery mess? Oh Jinsy, look there, right away as far as you can see – do you think that looks like a hill?'

'Yes,' said Jinsy, staring hard. 'Or no. Honestly, Sparrow, it could be a hill, it could be clouds.' 'Whatever it is,' said Krenn, 'there's all this marshland in the way.' 'Can't even paddle across it in a boat,' said Jinsy, 'much too muddy and tangled.'

'Even if we had a boat,' said Krenn.

'Could find one somewhere,' said Jinsy. 'Or make one. Should we go north, do you think, and find the open sea? We could look for a boat and go eastward that way for a bit.'

'I've never even seen the sea, and nor have you.'

'Always a first time!'

'Have you worked a boat, even?'

'Well no, not yet.'

'Nor me. I'd rather walk, if only there was anything to walk on.'

'Sparrow,' said Jinsy suddenly, 'use the Stone. Ask it where the paths are.'

'I can't! It shouldn't even be here!'

'How do you know? She could have meant you to have it, wanted me to bring it you.'

'You ought never have touched it!' cried Krenn wretchedly. 'I can't think why we haven't both been struck by lightning. And anyway you can't ask the Stone, Nanna always said it isn't a god, it's only a tool. It's not magic, it doesn't do tricks, it's holy. It's to help Her servants talk to Her.'

'I don't know who's Her servant at the moment if you aren't,' said Jinsy. 'You could have a try, Sparrow, you know you could.'

Krenn stared out at the watery wilderness ahead of her.

'All right,' she said at last. 'It can't make things any worse. You wait here, Jinsy, I'll go and find a place.'

Krenn walked past some tall oaks, made her way through tangled hawthorns and came to a yew tree. It bent right over, damaged in some storm perhaps, and made a dark green silent cave. This would do. She arranged some hawthorn twigs and berries in a circle and put the Stone, still wrapped, into the centre. Then she sat back on her heels and wondered what to do next. Unwrap it? She had still not actually seen the

Stone since Jinsy brought it to her, they'd neither of them dared unwrap it. Now she sang one of the songs her Nanna used to sing, a soft lilting melody, and then leaned forward and undid the coverings.

She had forgotten how beautiful it was. Dark, shiny, and with that little leaf-shape of brilliant white. Suddenly Krenn stopped being frightened and only remembered how much she had always loved the Stone, and her foster grandmother too, now gone away into the Lady's care. Nothing could change any of that. She picked up the Stone and laid it against her cheek.

Lady, she said in her mind, most holy and terrible Lady, I really didn't mean to. And don't take it out on Jinsy, he's only a boy, he doesn't understand. How could he?

Lady, I'm here, it's me, Krenn, I'm praying. What are we to do now? Which way can we go?

Am I to take it back?

Or go on?

But how? Where to?

Great Mother, why don't you tell me?

Nothing but silence. Krenn put the Stone carefully down again in the centre of the little circle, sat back on her heels and waited. Slowly, little by little, she began to feel calm, safe – there was the Stone in the ring of hawthorns, there was she in the green shelter of the yew tree – all the world enfolded in the Lady's care –

Then suddenly there were shouts, dogs barking, Jinsy's voice loud, angry – Krenn leapt up, grabbed the Stone and its wrappings and ran.

Now they go splashing across the Somerset Levels (but don't get me wrong, nothing was called 'Somerset' for thousands of years yet) and reach what is now Glastonbury, a holy place then, a holy place now.

CHAPTER FOUR
The Levels

Shouts, barking and laughter too. Krenn found Jinsy among a crowd of tall strangers, with one of them holding him by the shoulder and apparently much amused. Jinsy was unhurt, unafraid and furious. Krenn thrust the Stone out of sight inside her clothes, ran up to the man holding Jinsy and began to thump at him with her fists.

'Let him go!' she shouted. 'That's my brother, let him go!' One of the others laughed and took her by the neck with one hand and lifted her away. He shook her, set her down onto her feet, but kept hold.

'They took my knife!' said Jinsy furiously. 'My good flint knife, and my bow, and Shann's arrows, all of them, just grabbed them, look at her!'

The tall woman was turning the knife over and looking at it with amusement. She held it up to show the others, and they all laughed. Then she handed it to the man holding Jinsy, who smiled, stuck the knife into his own belt and then, apparently, said something to Jinsy.

Krenn was completely bewildered. Why was this man making those odd noises?

He made them again. The tall woman made some more. It sounded absolutely idiotic. Did they think they were talking, for goodness' sake?

Yes, yes they did.

'I can't speak their stupid language,' raged Jinsy. 'You'd think they'd know that. GIVE ME MY THINGS BACK!'

'You Must Let Him Go,' said Krenn, loud and clear as she could. 'And Give Us Back Our Knife! And the Bow, and the Arrows!'

She might just as well have been blowing bubbles into the air. No one heard her, no one noticed. All that happened was that the tall woman looked them up and down and said in her own language, 'Never in all my life have I seen such filthy children!'

'Will You Let Us Go?' insisted Krenn, but the woman only said,

'Someone wash them, at least! Then we can see if they're worth keeping. You, Sapri, take them down to that stream and scrub them.' The girl she spoke to took each of them by an arm and marched them down towards the water. They shouted and tried to twist away, but she held them firmly and got them to the water's edge.

'They fight,' she called back, laughing. 'Gorli, come and give me a hand!' Naturally they fought.

For all they knew, she could be going to drown them. Then they found they were only being washed, and stopped struggling and waited till it was over.

Sapri didn't just wash them. She called two more of her friends, got them to hold Krenn tight, and took a knife and hacked off most of her hair. Then she did the same to Jinsy. Krenn was hysterical with fury, she howled and shrieked, no one, but no one, ever had their hair cut off! What was she supposed to have done to deserve that?

But Jinsy had gone quiet. Suddenly he saw that the knife the girl was using was made of metal. Metal. He must be dreaming. No, metal it was, sharp and gleaming, just being used quite casually for cutting hair. It was only the second metal object Jinsy had ever seen in his life, the first being a copper dagger belonging to Hoony. It was Hoony's most treasured possession and had cost so many deerskins that the family had had to work all year to dress and finish them.

Sapri and Gorli finished cutting off his tangled locks and let him go. He shook his shorn head and ran quickly back from the water's edge to look at these new people. They were laughing and talking among themselves, amused at the fuss Krenn was making.

Jinsy stood and looked at them, counting. Stone axes, yes, and good ones, but what else? A man with a copper-headed throwing axe, one. Two with copper hunting knives, three. The women were wearing metal pins in their hair, not bone – say half a dozen, that made nine. The tall woman's belt had a metal clasp, ten. A dagger hanging from the belt, small, beautifully made, eleven. Jinsy put out his hand to touch it, and then drew back, but the woman unhooked it and held it out so that he could see. The man with the axe made some comment, and Jinsy looked at him again and saw that he had another piece of metal on him, but smaller and not copper. It was

a small round yellow disc and hung on a chain round the man's neck. Pretty, thought Jinsy, but not useful, must be some magic charm or other. He had no idea it was made of gold and had cost more than all the copper daggers and axes put together, nor that the plain cross pattern marked on it stood in the minds of these people for the god they worshipped. This was not the Lady, the Mother, goddess of the Moon, giver of life, but Her great and terrible child, the Sun.

'We'd never have got across this on our own,' said Jinsy.

'I suppose not,' said Krenn.

They were trotting across the marshes with the new people, not tied or held but definitely prisoners. If they slowed down or looked like striking off to the side, someone very quickly chivvied them on or thumped them back into line. They splashed through shallows, ran along mud banks, trotted in single file along heavy planks laid end to end or on bundles of sticks laid side by side on the surface of the bog.

'In the proper world,' said Krenn scornfully, 'the ground is there, you don't need to put all this rubbish down so as to get anywhere.'

'Clever, though,' said Jinsy, but Krenn didn't answer.

She hated the new people, she hated being a prisoner but most of all she hated the openness of where they were. All that space, all that sky. Under cover was so much safer.

The line of runners zigged here, zagged there, and made good progress. Bitterns boomed in the distance and pelicans flopped and splashed in the pools, shovelling up beakfuls of fish. Two herons flew across. After a while Krenn and Jinsy could see high ground rising up on the far edge of the marshes, a long low range of hills with a single towering little tump to its right.

'There you see,' said Jinsy, 'it wasn't cloud after all. And the world doesn't come to an end here, it goes on over there.'

'But can it be the Lady's world?' said Krenn anxiously, and Jinsy didn't know.

'We're going east, anyhow,' he said, 'and that's what you need to do. And these are very interesting people.'

'They are, are they?' said Krenn.

'Yes. Look at all those marvellous metal things they've got. And the clothes they wear! All patterned and full of colours.'

'Stolen, I expect. Like they took your bow and arrows and the knife.'

'They must know how to make those things,' said Jinsy. 'Someone must. Or where they grow. I wonder if we'll find out.'

Krenn didn't care whether they did or not. She

had had to leave the real world of hills and valleys, she had had her hair cut off, she couldn't bear the ridiculous babbling noises these new people made to each other, and on top of all that, there was Jinsy liking it! She ran and trotted across the wide splashy land in a state of cold despair.

The zigzagging tracks at last led them to the foot of the little hill on the far side of the marshes. There were houses there and more babble-talkers, all very glad to see Krenn and Jinsy's captors.

They stayed two nights there before going on with their journey. To Krenn's annoyance, Jinsy was by now getting on very happily with all these people. He learned their names and told them to Krenn – there were Sapri and Gorli, the two girls who'd given them their wash, the tall woman was Gacherray and the man in command of the party, the one with the copper axe and the yellow disc, was Echkan. There were three young men, Quarran, Ixtarry and Mel, and two boys, Arrizu and Ichuro, just old enough to count themselves men and take very little notice of two captured children.

'But they don't call themselves Echkan's people,' said Jinsy. 'They say they're Berren's people, and he lives a long way east of here, so we aren't stopping, we'll be going on soon.'

'How do you know?' said Krenn. 'How can you understand?'

'Easy,' he said. 'Pointing and that. And Gorli did a sort of this – high thing with her hands and said "Echkan", and then a much higher one and said "Berren! Berren!" as if he was someone who really mattered.'

'A long way east,' said Krenn thoughtfully. 'So it could be all right. But these are the wrong sort of people! Still, I suppose they could take us to the right place, even without meaning to.'

'What do you mean, wrong sort of people?' said Jinsy.

'My goodness Jinsy, can't you smell how wrong they are? Every one of them, the reek that comes off them, disgusting! And the worst thing, they don't worship the Lady. You can see them every morning at daybreak, see them and hear them! Men, only men, never any women. They sing songs to the sun, horrible songs! All jerky and noisy, but no one seems to take any notice of Her at all. That's awful!'

'Well – I suppose they just like the Sun best,' said Jinsy. 'They're doing what they think is right.'

'That's wicked!' said Krenn. 'And rubbish. The Lady rules all the others, we know that!'

'He's Her child,' went on Jinsy, trying to find

excuses for the new people. 'Perhaps She doesn't mind.'

'Her child, all right,' said Krenn, 'but so is every star, all the trees, the rivers – everything! All of them obey Her. He's just another one, that's all.'

There were no grey areas in Krenn's life, right was right and wrong was wrong and you pray to the Lady. Who else would anyone pray to? And men keep quiet and out of the way, only women dare talk to Her.

'It's a good place, this,' said Jinsy, chewing on a piece of dried fish. 'I like it. I like that stream that runs all red under the yew trees, and the way that little hill stands up so suddenly on the edge of all that flatness. I think this is a magic sort of place.'

'It's the wrong kind of magic,' said Krenn obstinately.

'Well, it hasn't done Berren's people any harm,' said Jinsy. 'Look how rich they are!'

'It won't last,' said Krenn. 'Ill-gotten gains do nobody any good, my Nanna always said so.'

'Oh Sparrow, you good little girl!' said Jinsy, laughing, and she threw a crust of bread at him.

CHAPTER FIVE

Without Spot
or Blemish

Echkan and his party spent a busy two days at the foot of the hill before going on with their journey. They drank from the red-running stream, they climbed the steep hill in the dark of the early morning to greet the rising sun, they danced in the spiral mazes that copied the circlings of the sun in the sky and trusted that this would encourage Him to come back every morning and not forget them. Only men and boys did these dances, not the women, and of course not Krenn or Jinsy, prisoners. Krenn heard the music they sang as they danced, and thought it was horrible.

Very early indeed on the second day, Jinsy and Krenn found themselves being led along between the round thatched houses by Gacherray. She stopped outside one of them, pushed them inside, said a few words and left them.

An old, old man sitting on a heap of furs spoke, and to their astonishment he spoke in their own language and they could understand him. He didn't speak it at all well, but it was good to hear it all the same.

He wanted to know their names, where they came from, and why. That was difficult, and the old man put it differently, why had they been sent out alone, so young? What had they done wrong?

'Nothing,' said Krenn, 'nothing. It wasn't that.'

'Then what was it? If not you, what had your people done wrong?' They looked at him blankly. 'I mean,' he went on, 'if you've done nothing wrong, then perhaps your people have, and they've decided to bind the wickedness on you and send you out into the forest. That way, you take it away from them. It can work very well, although it's more normal to use an animal, not a human, except for very serious offences.'

Neither Krenn nor Jinsy had ever heard of anything like this. There was nothing for it but to tell him the whole story from the very beginning when the squalling baby had been found in the forest and taken into Hoony's family for the sake of the Old Woman's daughter. The old man listened with interest, nodded as he heard about the far distant temple Krenn was to find, and didn't interrupt.

'And so,' said Krenn at last, 'Echkan's people found us on the far side of the marshes and made us go with them. And here we are.' She had been careful to say nothing about the Stone.

'Truly,' said the old man, 'the ways of the goddess are past finding out! Go in peace, my children.' They turned to go. Then,

'Father,' said Krenn hesitantly, giving him the most respectful title she could think of, 'do Berren's people worship the Lady?'

'Yes,' said the old man with a faint smile. 'Yes, and also no.'

'Oh thanks a lot!' breathed Jinsy, and Krenn hit him with her elbow.

'Certainly we reverence Her,' went on the old man, taking no notice. 'She is the Mother of all, the Giver of Life –' Krenn suddenly felt very much better – 'but chiefly we serve Her eldest child our lord the Sun who brings light out of darkness, joy out of sorrow, life out of death. There must be death,' he said firmly. 'The grain must die in the dark earth, the Sun must die each night in the west. The grain dies and gives new life. The Sun dies, and returns each day in splendour. Glory be to Him and to His holy Mother. Glory and praise.'

'Glory and praise!' echoed Krenn and Jinsy uneasily. The old man's head dropped forward and he fell into a doze.

The two children were just about to tiptoe away when he woke up with a jerk and said,

'Echkan will take you to the great temples of our lord the Sun in the very middle of the world. You are fortunate, both of you. The Lady has undoubtedly sent you to us. A gift to Her child.' He beamed at them happily. 'I will tell Echkan you are not wicked, and not carrying anyone else's wickedness. You are without spot or blemish. He need have no fears for the holy circle. Now you may go. The Sun and His Mother bless you.' This time he fell fast asleep and did not hear Krenn and Jinsy's subdued farewells.

'Holy circle?' said Jinsy to Krenn as they ran off. 'No fears about what?'

'How do I know?' she said.

'Well, it can't matter to us,' said Jinsy.

Oh no?

63

Echkan and his people and Jinsy and Krenn walked and trotted, trotted and walked, east, east and east, up hills, across streams, through woods, across clearings, river valleys, forest, forest and more forest.

'It's a relief to be back in proper country,' said Krenn to Jinsy one day, as the party dropped from a run to a walk. 'All that flat wet stuff, horrible. I wonder how much further we're going.'

'Two more days; I asked Mel.'

'Jinsy, how? You can't talk to them!'

'So who needs talk? All you want is fingers for counting, feet to tramp up and down for walking, and the round of the sky to point to for "days". Easy. I asked Mel, he doesn't mind taking time to make sure he understands.'

'You get on with them, don't you?' said Krenn accusingly. 'I believe you like them!'

'Yes, I do. The things they've got, the knives and clasps and all that, marvellous! But Ixtarry's a pain. Can't always dodge when he wants to thump you.'

Krenn jogged on and thought about the home she'd lived in so long but never belonged to. She wondered about Ensy. She knew very well that if the Old Woman of the family sinned against the goddess, it was the duty of the other women to punish her. She could be torn apart, torn into little bits, not enough of her left to be buried, no ceremony, no singing, no life to come, nothing. Or just turned out alone into the forest.

Krenn ran and trotted and felt the Stone in its bundle thumping gently on her back and hoped nothing terrible had happened to Ensy.

Nothing quite that terrible. Ensy was not dead, but that was the best anyone could say. She had lost Jinsy, her son. She had lost the Stone. The whole family was in shock, terrified, and they all watched her with a kind of numb despair, as if waiting to see how, if, she could ever bring the family and goddess back in touch again. How could life ever get back to normal? What hope was there for Sooral, now expecting her first child?

Jinsy's calculations had worked out just as he'd hoped. No one knew he'd gone until it was far too late to have any hope of finding him. No one realised that the little wrapped lump on a shelf in the Old Woman's hut wasn't the sacred and precious Stone of the Great Mother but an ordinary bit of rock smuggled in by Jinsy.

When Jinsy was missed, looked for and not found, and it was at last realised that he must have gone after Krenn, Ensy was wild with rage and blamed Krenn, but Haldo, Jinsy's father, told her it was nobody's fault but her own, and what did she expect, driving little Krenn out into the forest like that?

'So you keep the rules,' said Haldo angrily. 'All right, keep them, but when the goddess takes your son – my son! – don't blame young Krenn, blame yourself. Now will you get on with blessing the new homestead?'

'Yes,' said Hoony, stony-faced. 'Her priestess must sing the blessing. Must do it now.'

Ensy stood and looked at them both. Then she turned to the rest of the family and said, 'Very well then, into your places.'

They shuffled unhappily into line.

Ensy flung back her head, held the still wrapped stone high in both hands and prepared to begin the blessing dance. She let the wrapping fall off the stone – at once her fingers told her it felt wrong – her eyes told her it looked wrong – she couldn't believe it, it wasn't possible – then suddenly she realised, screamed, and flung the lump of rock away from her.

She screamed and screamed, others picked up the bit of rock, looked at it, threw it down again. A curse? Had it been changed by magic? What could have happened?

Always a quick thinker, Ensy recovered fast and gave nobody time to put the blame on her. Well aware of the danger she was in, she stopped screaming, grabbed a half-burned piece of wood out of the fire, whirled it round her head to make it blaze, and led off in a funeral dance. A lament for the Stone. Four steps and a stamp, four steps and a stamp, four steps and a stamp. Bit by bit they all joined in. No more hysteria, just a nice tidy funeral dance, singing as they went.

Then Ensy changed the step and the song. Six running steps, a left and a right, then the same again, all to a livelier tune, danced now under the new moon as it rose steadily in the sky. This was the blessing dance. They circled the hearths, the houses, the village, begged for the Mother's blessing on children, animals, hunting and crops. They asked for a kind winter and plenty of food, for the spirits of the dead to stay dead and not come back and play tricks, for the Stone to be put back into its proper shape, for health and wealth and plenty.

They danced and danced and danced, and when Ensy at last threw the smouldering branch onto the fire, Hoony's exhausted people sank down where they stood. After a while, slowly, they got the blessing feast together and began, unhappily, to eat it.

Where have Krenn and Jinsy got to? You'll have guessed by now, Salisbury Plain.

CHAPTER SIX
Berren's Ring

Echkan and the others reached home. All their neighbours and relations turned out to welcome them and there was feasting and singing because they had made the journey safely, sold their goods well in the west and brought home a rich load of precious tin. Also the two strange children. They were not tied up or shut in a shed, but they knew they were prisoners. No need to tie them up, where would they run to?

Gacherray's youngest daughter Gachi, a lively little person not more than four, took an instant liking to Krenn. She grabbed her by the hand and pulled her here and there all over the village, up past the smithy, down to the river, and showed her everything there was to see, talking all the time. Krenn didn't understand a word of it, but the little girl's good will was clear enough. Confused and homesick as she was, Krenn couldn't help being glad of it.

Then next morning, first thing, up the long hill, through the trees and up again onto a high cleared area – and the Stones.

They were so big that at first neither Krenn nor Jinsy could see them.

'Look!' said Gachi, pointing, 'look!' and,

'What? Where?' they said.

And then they saw.

As tall as trees, no, taller, taller than Jinsy or Krenn had any way of reckoning, almost two dozen towering blocks of stone loomed up above them, standing side by side in a curving row, making part of an enormous circle. Each was one single piece of stone. Each stood alone, a little apart from its neighbour, but joined to it by a great crosspiece, which lay like the lintel of a doorway across the tops of the stones.

'Doorways for giants!' said Jinsy. 'For gods! Wonderful!'

'No, terrible!' said Krenn. 'But how did they get there? Are they – are they alive? Can they move of themselves?'

Just then young Ichuro passed by, and laughed at the two children's amazement.

'Don't see anything like that where you come from, do you?' he said. 'Come on, foreigners, the holiday's over!'

Over it certainly was. Krenn and Jinsy and everyone else, young Gachi and the other small children too, all worked and worked and worked. If ever they slacked off, wiped their sweaty brows, paused to draw breath, Ixtarry or Mel or one of the others would shout a warning or crash a stick across their shoulders. Mel and Quarran mostly just shouted, but Ixtarry liked coming up quietly and using his stick.

What they had to do was simple enough – dig holes.

Huge enormous impossible holes, they were, placed neatly on the same curving line as the towering Stones, and Krenn was wondering what on earth they could be for, when she suddenly understood. They were the footings for more great Stones, more and more and more. It would make a circle.

Krenn saw now, or thought she did, why Echkan and Gacherray had been so ready to gather them up and bring them along from the west – Berren's people needed every pair of hands it could get, even childsized ones. Berren was building a temple to beat all temples, a ring of pillars, a dance of stones, a marker of the journeys of the sun and moon, the Great Ring of Berren. It would bear eternal witness, said Sapri, her eyes glowing, to the magnificence of the Lord Berren, whose name would live for ever, and to the glory of his god, the mighty, the terrible, bringer of light and life, lord of despair and darkness, master of all created things, the Sun! Right inside a vast and ancient moon temple of His Mother they were building Him a circle whose like had never been seen before and never would be again.

On and on it went. Down into the half-dug hole, hack at the chalky soil with a piece of deerhorn, scrabble and scratch and scrape, heave a full basket of rubble onto your back, up out of the hole, away through the gap in the embankment, scatter the rubble, go back to the hole, scrabble and scrape, load up again, climb out, take it away, tip it out, back to the hole – fill it up, tip it out, fill it up, tip it out, fill it up – the hole's deeper, nearly deep enough, they've brought a ladder, down it you go, dig and scrape, up again, slide down, scramble up –

Enough food, just. Enough water, just. Enough rest, no, not nearly.

Krenn and Jinsy had no word in their language for 'slave', because Hoony's people and the other forest families did not have servants, did not have slaves. It was not a word they could need. Everyone was family. But slaves are what Krenn and Jinsy were.

'And I could stand it better,' said Krenn desperately, 'if only they wouldn't keep telling us how lucky we are! At least I think that's what they're saying.'

'Such a privilege,' agreed Jinsy, 'to be serving their blessed Berren! He must be really someone, he must.'

'Their Lord Berren,' corrected Krenn, 'whatever that is! And we've never set eyes on him! How can we work for someone we don't even know?'

'Easily!' said Jinsy. 'Just keep on and on and on, dig scrape carry, dig scrape carry, dig scrape –'
'And why does he want all these terrible great things put up? I wish he didn't, they frighten me.'

'They frighten me too,' said Jinsy. 'But all the same they're wonderful.'

Krenn shook her head, puzzled and despairing. Another thing she couldn't understand in this new world was how bossy all the men were, all the boys too, and the women and girls seemed to think this was perfectly normal. Women were there to do what they were told, only men could talk to the gods, women stayed quiet, didn't matter, lucky to have the men to work for. Krenn felt uncomfortable all through her mind and body in such a wrong kind of place. The Lady must be furious.

After a while it was winter and all work on the digging stopped. Sleet and hail slashed across the village and the Stones, the river rose and ran thick and noisy, the days were short, dark and cold. Nothing more was done except the cutting and fitting of wooden stakes to line the inner faces of the huge empty holes still waiting to be filled. Sledgehauling of more giant stones from the north was also stopped, but the stone masons went on dressing the ones they already had. There were three of these, lying under shelters consisting of a single wooden wall and a thatched roof, so that work could go on in a good light and in all weathers. The clink-a-tink, clink-a-tink of stone on stone sounded all the daylight hours.

Jinsy was fascinated, and when he could get out of herding the pigs or frightening wolves away from the sheep – not often – he went to hang round the sheds, hoping to be allowed to help. But Chen, the head stonemason, was unshakeable.

'Can I give you a hand shaping that?'

'You couldn't lift the maul, boy.' That might be true. The maul was an enormous sandstone ball, Chen had to take two hands to it and even then it looked too big for him. All he did, or all he seemed to do, was to keep gently picking it up and letting it drop.

'It doesn't look difficult. It's not you doing anything, the maul does it.'

'That's right.'

'Can I try?'

'No.'

Chen was working on the most nearly finished stone, smoothing away all the few remaining roughnesses, getting a good final polish. The two knobs on the very top were as finished as they could be for the moment – one day they would fit into two corresponding holes hammered out of the undersides of the lintelstones, but all that could only be completed when the stone had been raised and set in place and had had time to settle into the ground. Jinsy fingered the knobs, and wandered across to where Mel was working on the lintel-stone.

'How do you know you've got those holes in exactly the right place?'

'You again?' said Mel. 'This will surprise you, boy – I measured.'

Jinsy flushed. Yes, of course. But all the same – Mel, do you know you haven't got this side dead straight up and down? It leans out.'

'Sun send me patience, boy! It's meant to lean out.'

'Oh, sorry. Why is it meant to, then?'

'I do believe we're running short of mauls. You just come here and let me twist that thick head of yours off and use it to shape –'

Jinsy ducked out of the way, laughing, and went back to watch Chen.

'Why does it, Chen? Have to lean out?'

'So's to look right from underneath, once it's up.'

'Oh. Chen, how many will there be altogether? Lintels and stones?'

'Thirty uprights. And more in the middle, set in a half circle.'

'And there's –' he looked round and counted – 'twenty up so far.'

'That's right. The twenty-first goes up next, three sevens, seven threes.'

'That's going there?' asked Jinsy, pointing to the hole he and the others had been digging last. Chen nodded. 'And that extra hole we had to dig, in front of it there, like a little grave, what's that for?' Chen glanced at him sharply and said nothing. 'Oh but Chen,' went on Jinsy, not noticing the old man's silence, 'it'll take you forever. Why can't I help?'

'Quicker without you. Besides, what's the hurry?'

'Well, I'd have thought –'

'Look, boy.' Chen paused with the great stone ball in his hands, set it down and straightened up to face Jinsy. 'Look around you.' He gestured with a sweeping arm at the wide stretches of upland slopes, the grazing land and forests that lay about them. 'Look at that. This is the centre of the world, the very centre. His holy place. We aren't building the Ring for you or for me or even for the Lord Berren, the Sun guard and keep him! We're building it for Him. In the exact centre of His world. And it will stand forever. For ever, if you can imagine that.' He bent down and picked up the maul again. 'What does it matter if it takes a few years more or a few years less? Now go and bother someone else, there's a good lad. Doesn't Quarran need a hand with the cows?'

Jinsy nodded and went away.

Even more attractive than the stonemasons' sheds was the smithy, where heat, hammering and water transformed dirty knobbly greeny-brown lumps into bright shining razor-edged knives, delicate pins and brooches, rich earrings and bracelets and fine little throwing axes. The mere sound of the place was magic – the roar of the furnace, the regular whumph-whumph of the bellows, the hammering, the hiss of water on hot metal. For a boy who had never known anything but stone tools, it was irresistible. But the smiths were very private people, they didn't like visitors.

Perhaps he could fetch wood for them, though, or work the bellows –

Jinsy ran down the hill and away to the river where Echkan's village stood close by the water, with the smithy at the far end.

Cambo and Ixo his elder son were working together at the anvil. Cambo was holding a piece of white-hot metal in a pair of long pincers, and the two of them were hammering onto it with alternate blows. Cambo looked up, saw Jinsy and jerked his head. Ixo put down his hammer and without a word used both his large strong hands to pick Jinsy bodily off the ground and fling him out of the smithy. Jinsy rolled as he hit the ground and was not badly hurt. As he got up, he glanced back and saw Ixo dusting his hands together and smiling. Smithing is for Smiths, Keep Out. Yes.

Well, there was always Sparrow. It was a long time since they'd had a talk.

Krenn and Gorli were pounding away at a tubful of grain, thump, thump, thump. Krenn's arms ached and her back was sore. She much preferred working at Gacherray's loom – a mind-blowing joy it had been, understanding at last how her own old piece of stuff must have been made, but when you're told to grind corn, you grind it.

And spinning, weaving, no amount of magical cloth-making could change anything – the little precious Stone of Hoony's people lay snugly against her side but heavily on her conscience. She ought to take it back. She had begged some pieces of leather, an awl and a needle from Gacherray and managed to make it a good carrying bag, a kind of satchel with a strong strap, but it needed more than that that, it should be washed, polished, sung to, revered. Everything was wrong here, all wrong.

Jinsy came and flung himself down beside them –

'Ouch, I'm sore! Oh Sparrow, Ixo's just thrown me out of the smithy, and I mean thrown. Crash, thump. Pity, because it's the most interesting place I've ever even dreamed of seeing. I wish they'd let me in.'

Krenn said nothing at all.

'Chen's much friendlier,' said Jinsy dreamily, 'but all the same he won't let me help. Marvellous, the way they plan those Stones and shape them! Sparrow, do you know, they have to cut them the wrong shape to start with, so that when they're up they'll look –'

'No!' flashed Krenn. 'I don't know and I don't

want to know and I hate them all and I hate you!
Just shut up, will you?'

Jinsy stared at her. Gorli glanced at them and
smiled. Quarrelsome little savages! What was
the child so cross about? Ah well, it wouldn't be
long now.

'Sparrow! How can you? I come out into the
forest to be with you, I leave all my own family,
even make myself the worst kind of thief and
take the –'

'Don't speak of it! Don't mention it!' Krenn
hissed in fury. 'It's holy, precious, and it ought
never have left its proper place! It's all wrong
here, wrong, wrong, and so are we, so are you!'

'Oh, very well If that's how it is! I do all I can
for you, and just because I have the sense to take
an interest in –'

'Jinsy, go AWAY! Now! Go away!'

Krenn rammed her grinding stone
down and down and down, hot tears
trickling down her face, and Jinsy
got up and stalked off, stiff-
legged and dignified. Gorli
looked at Krenn's working
face, but didn't speak.

Chapter Seven
Sacrifice

'Hey there, you, boy!' came Quarran's voice. 'What do you think you're doing, loafing around? You should be bringing in firewood. Go and find Arrizu, move!'

Jinsy turned and began to thread his way between the houses towards the woods. As he passed Gacherray's house he happened to hear his own name, and Krenn's. Then Sapri's voice saying,

'Such a pity, Gacherray, such a pity! I know they're slaves, but they're really nice children.'

Jinsy froze where he stood.

'All the better a sacrifice,' came Gacherray's voice. 'You don't give the gods rubbish. It has to be something we value.'

What in the name of the Holy Mother was she talking about? Himself and Krenn? Had he really understood her? He didn't always get this new language right. Jinsy drew closer to the thin walls of the house and listened with all his might.

'Yes, yes I suppose it does,' he heard Sapri say. 'And of course that's what we brought them here for, I know that. It would have been easier if we'd done it sooner, not had time to get to know them. But we had to wait for the holy time, for Midwinter.'

'Echkan would tell you it isn't supposed to be easy,' came Gacherray's voice. 'And it really is important. The holy circle must be exactly right, or the blessed Sun could turn away from us. And then just imagine what would become of us all!'

'I know, I know. And in any case the sacrifice is the Lord Berren's command. It's got to be done. I can't help being a bit sad, that's all.'

Gacherray gave a sigh and said, 'Yes, so am I. She's a dear child, I'm really fond of her. Do take care she doesn't find out yet, won't you? We can at least give her a happy time at Midwinter before she has to go under the knife.'

'Come down to the river, Sparrow,' said Jinsy. 'Something I want to show you.'

'I'm not talking to you,' said Krenn.

'Oh yes, you are. Come and see. It's important.'

Krenn glanced at him doubtfully, alerted by the tone of his voice.

'We've nearly finished this lot,' said Gorli, rubbing some of the meal between her fingers. 'You go off, the pair of you. May as well enjoy yourselves while you can!' she added, and Krenn thought nothing of it, while Jinsy shuddered.

They ran down to the river together. It was a late winter afternoon, cold but bright, and the last rays of the setting sun sent shafts of light between the bare trees. Jinsy took Krenn by the hand and pulled her towards an old oak tree that overhung the water.

'Up the tree,' he said. 'Go on, right up.'

'Jinsy, if this is some silly joke –!'

'No! No, Sparrow, not a joke. You'll see soon enough. Go on, right up, as far as we can get.' He spoke in a flat calm voice quite unlike his normal lively way, and it frightened Krenn. They climbed in silence. A squirrel chattered at them and scampered off in a flash of reddish fur.

'This'll do,' said Jinsy. 'They can't really see us and they certainly can't hear us. Sparrow, there's nothing to show you, that was just to get you away. Listen, listen and don't shriek or any thing – I overheard Gacherray and Sapri talking.'

'Well? Go on! What did they say?'

'They said – Sparrow, I've discovered why they brought us here from the west, what they mean to do with us.'

And he told her what he had overheard.

She believed him at once. Suddenly it all fell into place. 'Without spot or blemish' – a sacrifice has to be perfect. 'The Great Mother has undoubtedly sent you to us – Echkan need have no fears for the holy circle' – even, just now, Gorli telling them to enjoy themselves while they could.

'Yes, that's right,' said Jinsy. 'They said they wanted to make sure you had a really happy time at Midwinter. First. Before they do it.'

'Just me? Not both of us?'

'I think just you. Can't be sure.'

Krenn turned into Jinsy's arms and cried and cried. He held her close and waited. Recovering, she gave a great sniff, kissed him and sat up again.

'And I was very nearly beginning to like them!' she said. 'Horrible new people with the wrong language, wrong sort of songs and the wrong god! I was getting used to them! Wanting to be like them, learn how to spin, how to weave! Wanting them to think I was good at it!'

'Oh, they think you're great!' said Jinsy. 'Don't

worry about that! They were saying how sad they were, and that a proper sacrifice has to be something you really value.'

'Oh it does, does it?' said Krenn, turning fierce. 'So they'll kill me with the tears roIling down their faces, will they?'

'No!' said Jinsy. 'They won't kill you and they won't kill me, tears or no tears. We'll see to that!'

'Come on,' said Krenn, shifting on the oak tree branch. 'We've been up here long enough. We've got several days till their Midwinter. I'm hungry, let's go and eat.'

At the foot of the tree she paused, and added hesitantly, 'But Jinsy – my Nanna saw me making an offering, do you remember? But not my life, Jinsy, it can't have been my life!'

'No, my Sparrow, not your life.'

They ate very well. It was strange, wasn't it, the way everyone kept picking out the best bits and handing them to Krenn? She accepted them all cheerfully, and took care to share them with Jinsy, sitting close to her. He was very quiet, not his usual talkative self, but Krenn chatted and sparkled, using the new language in a way she had never done before.

She is fey, thought Gacherray anxiously, fey. Deep in her heart of hearts, she knows. Can she really know, has anyone told her? But then Krenn tossed off some laughing reference to a plant the new people didn't seem to know about, one she would find and show them in the spring, and Gacherray thought no, no, she doesn't know, she can't.

Lying wide awake that night, carefully silent because of all the others near her, Krenn slid her hand into the bag she had made for the stolen Stone, and held it. No one here had seen it, no one knew she had it, it was quite safe. But not cared for, not sung to, not playing its proper part in the family's life. How could they be managing without it? They need it for the blessing prayers, they need it if they're ill, I should have taken it back, she thought, taken it back at once. Or tried to, at least.

And where is She? The moon travels with you, go as far as you like through woods, across rivers, up hill and down dale and there She still is, somewhere and She always comes back, but now it's winter and keeps raining and She's always behind the clouds, I can't see her, She doesn't want me any more.

Lady?

Do you remember when I tried to pray and then they came and laughed at us and took us prisoner?

Why did you bring me here?

What am I to do?

But then she fell asleep.

'Wait,' said Gacherray next morning. 'You need something better to wear. The Lord Berren will be here tonight, there'll be feasting and songs, dancing, I must find you something pretty.'

Pretty to be killed in? thought Krenn. Kind of you! Aloud she only said,

'Oh good, thank you. I've worn this old piece of cloth just about all my life, and it does look like it. Though I'm glad you've shown me how to make more like it, I really am.' And then she added, 'Gacherray, there's feasting tonight for the Lord Berren, but when exactly is the festival, the Midwinter? It's only half moon now, do you have it at full moon?'

'Nothing to do with Her,' said Gacherray,

fingering the brown and tan striped material Krenn was wearing as a kilt. 'It's the festival of the Lord Sun, on the shortest day of the year, when the darkness nearly conquers. A very dangerous time. We light fires and we dance, of course, and make offerings – yes, make offerings, and then if the Lord Sun accepts the offerings He comes back to us, darkness is defeated, light and warmth return. This is good cloth you're wearing, Krenn, and an unusual pattern, just rather old, a bit shabby. It reminds me of something.'

'I was found wrapped up in it when I was a baby,' said Krenn. 'My Nanna used to say what a clever thing it was, we don't use anything like that, just properly dressed skins.'

'I know what it reminds me of!' said Gacherray. 'It's very like a pattern my sister used to weave. Well now, let's see what we can find for you.'

Together they rummaged through a basket of fabrics, and Gacherray thought about her sister Lacarren, dear Lacarren, who had once been Berren's chief wife. She was a stubborn girl, not to say pig-headed, and had insisted on going travelling when she was far too heavily pregnant and had died in childbirth a long way from home. Years ago, it was, but Berren had never really got over it, although he had several excellent wives now and a host of healthy children. Indeed, life is full of unhappiness. What's another death or two when you count it all up?

'Look,' she said, 'here's a very nice piece of yellow with a red stripe. Would you like me to make something up out of that? The Lord Sun's own colours! I can do it quite quickly if you would. Then you'll look just right for the Midwinter festival.' Krenn smiled and thanked her and said yes, she would.

'But I wish you prayed to the Mother!' Krenn added. 'Isn't there anywhere near here that belongs to Her, anywhere you can go to talk to Her?'

'The whole place belongs to Her in a way,' said Gacherray, looking puzzled. 'You know the Lord Berren's new temple for Her child, for the Lord Sun, that's being built inside an old one of Hers.'

'She can't like that very much,' objected Krenn. 'Isn't there anywhere that still belongs just to Her and no one else?'

'Well, yes, I suppose there is. About a day's walk to the north of us, a long day's walk, there's the Old Ring, a huge temple, very old and holy, where they still worship Her, won't have anything to do with the Lord Sun, if you can believe it! And there's another close to it, a tiny one, even older I think. But your legs aren't long enough and it's too far in midwinter, don't even think of it!'

'No,' said Krenn obediently. 'No, I'll go there in the spring, or when I'm older.'

'You do that, dear,' said Gacherray, trying to smile, and she ran the red-striped cloth through her hands, remembering Lacarren.

On the move again, northwards. To Avebury. And Echkan's village, by the way, is Amesbury, the place where they found that princely burial not long ago. I don't like it when they dig people up, I'd rather they left them in peace, but you can't help being interested.

CHAPTER EIGHT
Sanctuary

Next morning –

'They aren't watching us, they think we don't know, we can slip off any time.'

'As early as possible,' said Krenn, slinging the holy Stone in its satchel carefully over her shoulder and checking that the strap was secure. 'So as to have plenty of daylight.'

'Now?'

'Now.'

'But separately, safer like that. Meet you – oh, meet you upriver where the brook comes in.'

'Yes, that'll do,' said Krenn. 'Bring all the food you can.'

'Everyone's busy getting the Berren feast ready, there ought to be pickings.'

There were. Well laden, well wrapped up, Krenn wearing Hoony's deerskin cloak over everything and hugging the Stone in its bag close to her side,

the two of them slipped by different paths out of the cluster of houses and met as arranged.

Even in the middle of winter, there was no problem knowing which way was north. If the sky had not shown it clearly, the tracks would have done, for this was the way many of the huge heavy stones were dragged down from the country near the Old Ring. They had been lying about up there since the world began, and all this past summer they were being hauled and manhandled on rollers or on slipways and pulled by sweating teams of men and women to Berren's land, where he was building his Great Ring. No one could mistake the way.

Jinsy and Krenn ran, walked, ran again, dodged other travellers if they saw them in time, greeted them cheerfully if they didn't, and once caught sight of a bear shambling off into the undergrowth.

No one was tracking them, they weren't missed until evening and by then they knew they could not be far from the Great Mother's oldest Ring. But it was dark, too dark to go on, and they climbed into the leafless branches of an oak tree and prepared to wait it out until dawn. It would be cold through the night.

Trumpets sounded in the woods outside Echkan's village, trumpets and horns, a loud joyful blaring sound.

'He's here, he's coming, he's here!' people

shouted, and poured out through the trees to meet him. A surprisingly small man, glinting with gold, Berren of the Ring walked at the head of his war-band into Echkan's village. His smile would charm the birds off a tree or any woman into his bed; when he frowned, people went very quiet. Two tall hunting dogs paced sedately at his side, a smaller terrier-like dog trotted ahead of them.

Echkan flung himself down to kneel at his lord's feet, then jumped up laughing and offered him the traditional loaf of bread and flask of wine. Laughing too, Berren drank from the flask, then handed it back to Echkan, tore off a piece of bread and began to eat it.

'And how I need it!' he said. 'Finish the wine, Echkan, but leave me the bread!' He broke off pieces and handed them to his followers, then gave some to the dogs, Harren, Etchegay and Larrok. 'On the road since before sunrise and hardly a bite to eat! This is Gacherray's making, isn't it? Yes, thought so, nothing like it.'

'There's a very considerable feast being got ready for you,' said Echkan, falling into step beside Berren. 'You won't go hungry for long.' Then he added, 'You'll stay with us, Lord Berren, won't you? Over the Midwinter festival, I mean. And offer the sacrifice for the holy circle?'

'Echkan, indeed I will. Who should do it, if not I? A circle for the Sun, yes, but they will call it Berren's Ring till the end of time! And the sacrifice itself, your messenger told me you've found a suitable child down in the west and brought her here. Is that correct?'

'Yes, a girl, a foundling I believe, no one claims her. The priest at the Red Brook talked to her, he guarantees that she's good in every way, thoroughly fit for our needs.'

'So I was told. Good. Tell me, does she know yet that she's to die?'

'No. No, we – well, Gacherray took a liking

to her – we all did – you'll see for yourself, she's an attractive child, full of character. Gacherray wants to give her a happy Midwinter. Weakness, Lord Berren, I admit!' Berren smiled.

'You softhearts! It has to be done, you know it has. Stones and sweat and labour, they are useless without the ultimate offering, the innocent blood freely poured. Twenty stones raised already, the twenty-first next, this is the right time to do it. And, Echkan, you ought to know, it's only a true sacrifice when you give something you like, love even. There's no palming Him off with second-best.'

'I know that, indeed I do. Don't worry, the child will be there.'

That evening, supper time. The party in full swing. The Lord Berren and the dozen men he had brought with him laughing, talking, singing, jumping up to join in the dances, celebrating. Old friends delighted to see each other again. Not one but half a dozen cooking fires burning steadily, rich smells of good food, stars and the half moon hazy behind clouds.

'Midwinter Eve tomorrow,' said Berren, stretching lazily. 'Time for the women to go out and gather greenery, dress the houses, dance the blessing. In and out and roundabout! Next day we do the Sun Dances round the Stones and God willing He hears us and begins to come back to us. And the day after that, the death for the holy circle. A busy and blessed time!' He finished biting the meat off a chop bone and tossed it to his terrier, Larrok, who took it away into the shadows. The two big dogs turned their elegant heads to watch, but did not condescend to show any real interest. 'By the way, which one of the children is she, this girl from the west? Point her out to me.'

'There are two of them,' said Echkan, looking about him. 'A foster brother. Mel, Quarran, where's the boy Jinsy? Gacherray, where's Krenn?'

No one had noticed them lately. No one had seen them for some time. No one had seen them all day.

Black as thunder, Berren sent out runners. Pitch dark now, beginning to rain, the moon invisible behind thick cloud.

No news, no sightings. Travellers who had come into the village were questioned. No, no one had noticed two children, unaccompanied, no.

Gacherray had known Berren all her life, he had dearly loved her sister Lacarren, but even she had to take her courage in both hands before she dared speak to him. Should she tell Echkan and get him to talk to Berren, do it that way? No, she would do it herself.

'Lord Berren!' He turned a dark gaze on her but said nothing.

'Lord Berren, two things. I believe I may know where the children have gone. And I am beginning to think that the girl is Lacarren's child. Lacarren's and yours.'

Still he stared at her and did not speak.

'The cloth, the pattern, Lacarren's weave –' Gacherray explained. The pattern she had recognised in Krenn's kilt – why, those people down in the far west don't even weave, just wear skins, they never made this! How the child had been found wrapped in it as a baby, in that very part of the country, at that very time – Gacherray had been thinking and thinking, weeping and worrying. Now she was sure. She trembled with emotion as she said, 'Lacarren made that piece of cloth. Krenn is my dead sister's child, my niece. Your daughter.'

'The Lord Sun demands that I kill my

daughter?' said Berren at last in a low voice. 'My own child?'

'How can we know?' said Gacherray, sweating with relief and fear.

'I have done it once, I suppose,' he continued thoughtfully. 'If you are right. When we buried Lacarren and left the infant in the forest. With Lacarren dead, how could it have lived? But now, am I to take her life again?' 'A truer sacrifice if you give something you like, love even.' His own words to Echkan echoed in his mind. Had the Lord Sun saved the child years ago, so that she could be offered to Him now? Or had the Lady saved her, for whatever reasons of Her own?

'She must be found. The boy too. You said you knew where they had gone. Where?'

'Where they might have gone,' corrected Gacherray. 'North, to the Lady's place, the Old Ring.' And she told him how Krenn had been asking her if there weren't a temple somewhere near that belonged to the Lady and no one else.

'Send the best runners north,' said Berren. 'Ixtarry and Quarran, aren't they? Who else, Echkan?'

'Mel is even faster,' Echkan answered, 'and more observant. Better at tracks. Or they may well be going west, trying to get back to their homeland.'

Quickly Berren ordered other runners off in other directions, and then went by himself up the hill to the Stones, his face grim.

Clouds scudded across the dark sky. A half moon gleamed fitfully through them, and Berren cast it an anxious, almost resentful glance. He began to walk slowly right round outside the great circle, touching each stone as he went and muttering a prayer to the Lord Sun. Then, having walked all the way round, he went in amongst the Stones and stood beside the small newly dug grave. Empty.

The Ring for the Lord Sun must be perfect.

Lord Sun, will you drink her blood? It is my blood too, mine and Lacarren's.

The child serves Your Mother. Surely She will give You whatever you ask.

How can I tell what She wants? What You want?

He knelt down, crouched forward, head in hands, as low as he could get before the terrible Lord he served, light, life, warmth and growth, who could burn, devastate and kill.

Tell me, tell me.

Clouds rolled and parted, gathered and dispersed again. Through a gap in them shone the light of the waxing moon. Its rays blazed out in the darkness and for some moments cast shadows of the great Stones across the trodden earth, the deeply sunk holes and the little grave. Berren raised himself up, sat back on his heels and watched. Somewhere a fox barked and an owl hooted. The grave stayed dark, shadowed, the moonlight refused to touch it.

Stiffly Berren got to his feet. He had had his answer. Now he had to decide what it meant. He was a man who normally knew exactly what to do next, and not being certain made him uncomfortable and angry. His dogs rose and trotted after him down to the village.

Next morning, chilled and stumbling, Krenn and Jinsy climbed down the oak tree and headed north again. A faint star still shone in the pale sky, but daylight was on its way.

So were Berren's runners, and so now was Berren himself.

'Look!' cried Krenn. 'That low round building across on that hill, is that it?'

'I hope so,' said Jinsy. 'Let's find out,' and they began to run. Then they heard a shout behind them, glanced back and settled down to run ten times as hard. Three men were hunting them, one in the lead and then two side by side.

'It's Mel,' panted Jinsy, 'running in front. Quick, give me the Stone! Don't argue, give. And then run on.'

Who could she trust if not Jinsy? Krenn held it out wordlessly without letting her stride falter, and Jinsy took it, held securely as it still was in its satchel. Then he stood suddenly aside and keeping hold of the carrying strap, he flung the Stone knee high at Mel with all the strength in his body. The strap whirled tight round Mel's legs and brought him crashing down

Well done, the Lady! thought Jinsy to himself, as he hastily shook the Stone free of Mel's legs, then turned to race after Krenn. But he found his ankle gripped, gripped and held. Mel lay flat, winded, but had reached out a hand and held him. Screaming with anguish, Krenn darted back, took the precious Stone from Jinsy's hands and escaped into the tiny ancient temple.

'Hold this,' she cried, 'hold it!' pressing the Stone into the hands of the astonished young woman who stood there. Then she stood in the gateway with tears pouring down her face and tried to make herself go back to help Jinsy. She wept aloud and struggled to make her legs move, but they stayed just where they were. She could not do it.

The other two men were coming up now. Mel rolled over and sat up, still fighting for breath. 'Get my knife, Sparrow!' shouted Jinsy.

'Get my knife!'

Suddenly the terror dropped away, Krenn could move again, and she raced to her foster-brother, picked up the stone dagger from the ground where the impact of Jinsy's fall had flung it and began to saw at Mel's wrist with it. He yelled out at the pain and grasped her with his other hand.

'Worse,' panted Krenn, 'worse! Jinsy, get free!' Together the two children fought, bit, head-butted, writhed and wrestled, flung up their arms and slid downwards – and escaped.

Furious, Mel got onto his knees, still coughing, almost black in the face, with nothing in his hands but scraps of Krenn and Jinsy's clothes. Scowling, he wrapped a piece of rag round his bleeding wrist, glared towards the temple gateway – those damned imps were still there, looking out at him – and turned to swear at the other two runners who now trotted up, cool and unhurried.

These two were Quarran and Ixtarry. They were sorry to have missed the encounter but saw no problem; the children couldn't stay in this small temple forever. Just a question of waiting. Ixtarry and Mel stayed on guard and Quarran began to run back to find Berren and report.

'Don't worry,' said the young woman, who was also Old Woman of this Ring, putting an arm round each of the shivering children, 'This is the Lady's house. No one can come in, no one. You are quite safe.'

CHAPTER NINE
Midwinter

'But he can talk people into anything,' said Krenn some time later. 'He's – he's a very magic kind of man.'

'We'll see about that, shall we?' said the young priestess, and smiled.

Quarran ran and ran, reached Echkan's village, found the Lord Berren still dark and thoughtful from his prayers in the Great Ring, and made his report.

'And Mel and Ixtarry are on guard, you say?'

'Yes, Lord.'

'Nothing gets past them, good. I can put my hand on the children whenever I like. Quarran, dismiss. You've earned a rest. Send Echkan to me.'

'Lord.' Quarran bowed, and trotted off.

'There's no hurry, Echkan,' Berren said to him

when he came. 'They can't escape, we can take them any time. But of course we need them tomorrow for the ceremony. Send a couple of men now to relieve Mel and Ixtarry, and I'll get there myself as soon as I can.'

'He can't come now,' said the young Old Woman. It was Midwinter itself, the shortest day of all the year, dark and cold. 'They have to dance the Sun Dances and go in and out and round about those wonderful Stones the Lord Berren is putting up, all sorts of things they have to do, and the Lord Berren himself must do them. He won't come here today. We'll go down together to the Old Ring, the Great Ring – have you seen it?'

No, they had come straight here, safe into the Lady's keeping.

'Then it will surprise you,' promised the girl. 'There are parts of it men don't go into, of course, but you come too, Jinsy, most of it's open to all Her people. Bring the Stone, Krenn.'

'Mel and Ixtarry aren't there any more,' said Jinsy, who had been peering out close by the gate. 'But there are two others.'

'Only two?'

'Yes, I think so.'

'And they're together?'

'Yes.' The girl laughed.

'Do they really think there's only one way in and out? Come on, this way.' She led them across to the opposite side of the little building and took hold of what looked like a piece of wattle fencing. She gave it a push, it pivoted and let them out into the open, with the building still between them and Echkan's two men. Down the hill they went, across the brook and towards the Old Ring.

Krenn danced her way down the hillside. She was like a new creature that morning. She had told the Old Woman everything that had happened, she had knelt in the Great Mother's tiny and holy house and sung the proper songs for the sacred Stone; she felt safe and cleansed. Decisions could wait. Perhaps she could go home and show Sooral and Sarren how to manage a spindle and distaff, how to weave the thread into cloth. They would like that, and Ensy would hate it, and in no time at all would be better at it than any of them and telling them they were doing it wrong!

Huge massive ramparts shone white in the winter morning sunshine and Krenn and Jinsy stopped in their tracks and stared.

'It still takes my breath every time,' said the young Old Woman, smiling. 'Now we go in this way, come along.' The high white walls towered above them, and Krenn and Jinsy went where they were led, in a daze of astonishment. 'A white Ring for the Moon, you see,' said the Old Woman, and turned to lead them into it.

'Chalk,' said Jinsy, fingering the face of the wall. 'They built these enormous walls and then finished them off with chalk.' He licked his finger and rubbed it against the surface; yes, chalk.

It was a vast circle, enormous, far bigger than the Great Ring of Berren. Not so tall, but much, much wider. You could have put his Stones in there half a dozen times and still had room. Four roads led off to the east and west, the north and south. These ran out through four great gateways cut in the enclosing ramparts.

'Later,' said the Old Woman, 'at the right time of the year, the Lord Sun sets exactly there,' and she pointed to the western gateway. 'As he touches the edge of the world, he fills that gap exactly and shines his blessing into His Mother's holy Ring. And the blessed Moon – well,' she laughed, 'it would take too long to explain it all to you! Look, and you'll see what I mean.'

They looked at the whole strange complex of giant stones, jagged and rough, the series of patterns and circlings, enclosed within the enormous ramparts, and were lost for words.

'They show the movements of the blessed Moon, the dances of the Sun and the stars – it is a lifetime's study!' said the girl cheerfully. 'Come in with me and meet the Old Woman of this Ring.'

In the holiest part of the greatest Ring ever built for the blessed Moon, Krenn knelt next day and offered up the tiny sacred Stone of Hoony's people. Shaking with emotion, she set it carefully on a small stone altar and then sank her head onto her arms and burst into tears. The young Old Woman started forward to comfort her, but the priestess of this Ring, a solid and formidable lady, put a hand on her arm and held her back.

'Let her cry it out, let her finish,' she said.

Jinsy stood back out of the way, behind a barrier that kept out boys and men. Waiting, still overawed by the size and splendour of this Ring, he stared across at the distant entrance gate, the one that faced towards the west, homewards.

People were coming in, pilgrims and travellers,

people coming to pray. He watched first one group and then another. Some of them reminded him of his own family and he felt a pang of homesickness. This wandering had gone on long enough, but how could he ever go home? No, he had chosen Sparrow and that was that.

Krenn stopped crying, raised her head and rubbed her eyes, then got to her feet and turned towards the two Old Women.

'What should I –?' she began, and then gasped, exclaimed, and began to run.

Ensy, Haldo and Shann were walking in through the western gate.

'Krenn, where's Jinsy?' It wasn't what Ensy had meant to say. Where's the Stone? or You wicked girl, how could you? But no, 'Where's Jinsy?'

'He's here, look, just over there, he's all right. Oh Ensy, Ensy! I mean, Old Woman!' And Krenn flung herself into Ensy's arms and Ensy received and hugged her. It would be difficult to say which of them was more surprised.

'The Lord Berren wants them back, though,' said the younger Old Woman a little later on when all the hugging and exclamations were done for the moment. 'The girl especially. And he'll be here before long. This will be difficult, and –'

'But Krenn,' said Ensy, not caring a row of beans for any lordberrens, 'what did happen to the Stone? Do you know? Did the Lady change it into that lump of rock or did you take it when you went away? It has been terrible without it, terrible!'

'It's here, it's here, safe and cared for. Did you come here to look for it? I should have brought it back!'

'Yes, to look for it, and for you. Sooral said – well, Sooral and some of the others too, they said I should never have sent you away, that everything that happened after you'd gone was my fault. Pigs dying, Sooral's baby so ill –'

'Sooral has had her baby! And it's ill? A boy or a girl? Old Woman, how ill is it?'

'Very ill,' said Ensy soberly. 'A boy. He looked just like Jinsy when he was born. Not any more, though, too thin, wasting. The Lady is very angry; anyone can see that. So we have come here, to Her holiest place, to beg Her forgiveness, to ask for help.'

'The Stone, it's here,' Krenn said again. 'I

couldn't think what else to do, so I offered it, this temple's got it now.'

'In trust only,' said the Old Woman, following closely. 'In trust. It must go back to you.' She went straight to the little altar, laid a cloth over the dark shining Stone and picked it up and put it into Ensy's hands. 'I give it to you now. May Her blessing go with it. May the child and the mother do well.'

'Arrows,' said Jinsy suddenly, 'arrows. I'll make another lot, Shann, really I will,' and Shann shouted with laughter and said he would let him off this time.

Krenn could not bear it – she jumped up and did handsprings all the way round her rediscovered family until she collapsed on the ground beside them, dizzy and laughing.

She was still sitting sprawled on the ground with a silly smile on her face when she saw Jinsy and the others draw together and stare anxiously towards the southern gate. The Lord Berren had arrived.

CHAPTER TEN
Andal

Face to face in the outer courtyard of the Old Ring, Berren and Krenn stared at each other. Close beside her, braced to defend her, stood Jinsy. Behind him were his brother and parents. At Berren's back were a number of his men, armed and dangerous. Echkan was there, so were Ixtarry and Quarran and Mel too, his wrist bandaged and his face dark. The two priestesses stood a little aside, watching.

Berren knew he had to persuade Krenn out of the holy temple. She was as safe there in the Lady's house as if – as if she were sitting perched up on the crescent moon itself, looking down and laughing at him. He could not use force there, only persuasion.

'Come home!' he said with a sudden melting smile. 'Come home to us, your family, your own people! The Stones and the houses are decked with greenery, you've missed all the blessing dances and the Sun Dances and the feasting. Come back while the holly and the ivy are still green and there's plenty of food and drink left, more dancing to do, more songs to sing. Come home!'

'You meant to kill me,' said Krenn. 'Eight years ago down there in the west you put me out to die.'

'I did,' he agreed. 'As my Lacarren had died. You would have gone to her. You know I had to do that, what else was there?'

Krenn nodded; she did know. She stared at this strange man and thought: That's my father. Why don't I feel anything?

How alike they are! thought the girl priestess, watching. Lady, help them do right! She stood still as a stone and prayed with all her strength.

'But what about now?' asked Krenn. 'What about the death for the great circle?'

'Ah, so you knew that too!'

'It wasn't difficult.'

'An honour,' said Berren earnestly. 'A great and serious honour. To give your life for the Lord Sun's glorious temple, could anything be more wonderful?'

'Yes!' Ensy stepped forward. 'Yes. To grow up and love and be loved and bring children into the Lady's world.'

'And you are –?' asked Berren loftily. 'I do not expect to discuss matters with women.' Certainly not with this lean, travel-worn primitive from the back of beyond.

'My name is not spoken. I am Old Woman of our people. I stand for the Lady. So do my two sisters here. Krenn is the Lady's child and you may not touch her.' The Old Woman of the White Ring nodded, and she and the young priestess moved a little to stand beside Ensy.

Trouble on my very doorstep, thought Berren. Not wise. Offending the Lady Herself, dangerous. What does the Lord Sun want? he thought with sudden fury. Why can't He tell me?

Then, with relief, he knew. He thought back over his prayers, the moon-shadow and the light and darkness, and he knew. The answer shone clear as moonlight in his mind. He smiled lovingly at his daughter and said,

'Child, I am not going to kill you twice. I prayed about this, I prayed and prayed, and now I know that once is enough. I knelt among the Stones, among the shadows they cast, knelt beside the new grave, and the Mother's light refused to touch it. She rejects it. She does not want it. I am not required to lose you a second time. The Lord Sun will provide another sacrifice. Come home with me, come home to Gacherray and young Gachi, your own family, and you will be safe. Do you believe me?'

Slowly Krenn nodded. Yes, she did believe him. No, she did not know what to do.

And anyhow, did she have a choice? Berren might be asking her kindly now, honey-sweet and tender, but how long would he stay sweet if she refused?

And what about Jinsy? Did she dare ask?

'Lord Berren, what about Jinsy? You say I'm safe, and I – yes, I believe you. Is he?'

'If you want him, yes.'

Krenn felt totally confused. She was sure of only one thing in the world – that she must take back the Stone. It should never have left Hoony's people. How could they pray without it? Plant the crops, heal the sick, lay the dead to rest?

Berren stood waiting, silent. How like Lacarren the child looked! He was in no doubt of her answer.

Krenn could not speak. She looked at Ensy, and took her hand.

Ensy held it firmly and said, 'You cannot have her. She is not *krenn* any more, she is *andal*, beloved. And after so long, and so much happening, she belongs to us. She always did, if I'd only seen it.'

Berren looked at Ensy, Haldo and Shann as if they came from a different species. He was dealing with people who had never heard of him, who had no idea of lords and servants. They neither knew nor cared how important he was, and Berren found it baffling. Very quiet and controlled, he explained patiently that Krenn – oh all right, Andal – was his own daughter. No, certainly, he had no intention of sacrificing her, not now, hadn't he just said so? He would find an alternative. No, all right, not Jinsy either. But to his total amazement they simply kept saying, in effect, Well, so what?

When people don't respond to your threats or your promises, what do you do? Berren glanced at Echkan, and he and his men drew in and formed a closer circle round the little group.

'You will not use force, my lord,' said the Old Woman of the White Ring calmly. 'Not in here. Not in Her holy place.'

Krenn stood huge-eyed and amazed, listening.

'My dear people,' said Berren yet again, 'you don't understand. I am Berren. This is my child.'

'Rescued and raised by us,' said Ensy.

'My good friends,' he cried, turning on them all the charm he possessed, 'you haven't thought, you haven't considered! The child is my child, bone of my bone, flesh of my flesh. The time and place prove it, Lacarren's length of cloth proves it, Krenn's smile alone proves it! It is beyond dispute.'

Charm cut no ice with Ensy. 'We don't dispute it,' she said. 'We simply tell you it doesn't matter.'

'In the name of the great Sun, I tell you –' exclaimed Berren, blazing suddenly, but Ensy flashed straight back,

'And in His Mother's greater name, I say this child is ours!' If she hadn't been so desperately concerned, Krenn could have laughed.

At this point Jinsy bravely interrupted,' 'Lord Berren, you were going to kill her, you know you were.'

'She is my daughter,' said Berren, flushing darkly, 'and that is my business.' But then he decided to be patient a little longer and said in a more friendly voice, 'There's no need for us all to stand here and shout. Let's sit down and discuss the matter quietly.'

They settled themselves in a ring, Echkan with Mel and the other men still standing round them, ready if their lord signalled. Shann, too, stayed on his feet, guarding his family's back, and Jinsy stood beside him. Haldo half-knelt beside Ensy.

The will of the god.

The will of the goddess.

She is mine.

She is ours.

I loved her mother.

We love her.

On and on it went.
Then there was silence.
No one would give in. No one had anything fresh to say.
Berren got to his feet and glanced at Echkan. No need to hurt anyone. Mustn't use violence in the Lady's house. You hold them here, I pick her up and go. They had worked together so

long, they didn't need words. Echkan nodded and put his hand on his sword-hilt. Haldo and Shann were alert at once. At this point the young priestess spoke.'

'Will you listen to me?' Everyone turned to look at her. 'This child, Andal, carried the holy Stone of Hoony's people, tended it and cared for it. Even by accident, even by theft she is therefore a priestess of the Mother. You must ask the Mother's servant which she prefers. Ask Andal.'

Jaws dropped and mouths fell open, Krenn-Andal's as well.

Jinsy recovered first.

'A very good idea,' he said. 'Tell them, Sparrow.'

'Yes, my daughter,' said Berren, smiling. 'Tell them.'

Both families want me. No one ever did before. Both of them nearly killed me. Not much of a choice, really. I belong to both of them. To neither. To myself, that's all.

She looked round at all their attentive faces – Berren, wonderful, dangerous – Haldo and Shann, uneasy – Ensy, scowling – Jinsy, agonized – oh no, she had no choice to make, no choice, it made itself.

Krenn went across to where Berren was

standing. He opened his arms wide and she went into them, laid her head on his chest and found that she was crying.

'That's my darling,' he said, holding her close. 'Don't cry, don't cry! Think how glad little Gachi will be to see you, and Gacherray, your own aunt.'

But Krenn dried her eyes, reached up to kiss him and stepped back. 'No,' she said, 'that was goodbye. Give my best love to Gachi, and to all of them. Tell them I'd like to come and see them sometimes, now I know the way. May I do that?'

'My darling, why?'

Krenn made a despairing gesture. How could she explain? She didn't really know why herself.

'I belong where I'm used to, I suppose. Now that they want me. They serve the Lady – and – well, I know the songs there.'

'The songs?' said Berren blankly.

'Yes. They're all the wrong tunes, the songs you sing to the Lord Sun. The Lady's are the proper ones.'

It was the songs did it. The songs, and the fact that Berren was a truly great man. He knew when he had lost and could accept defeat. Now he smiled at his daughter, kissed her and led her across to Ensy.

'Take good care of her!' he said. 'I shall come and make sure you do.' Then he lifted a gold sun-disc off his own neck and put it round Krenn's, unhooked a precious bronze dagger from his belt and handed it to Jinsy, jerked his head to Echkan and his other men and went. Another sacrificewould the Lord Sun accept the slaughter of his best hunting dog? Did that mean Harren, or Etchegay? He wasn't sure if he could do it. Little Larrok? Lord Sun almighty, how many dogs equal one human?

It was very quiet after he had gone.

'Oh Sparrow,' said Jinsy, 'oh Sparrow. I thought you'd chosen him.'

'Never,' she said, gripping his hand, 'never. Ens – Old Woman, when can we start for home?'

'The sooner the better,' said Ensy. 'Getting on for full moon, so that's good, and how they can be managing without the Stone! We must get it to Sooral as fast as we can. And weeds grow even in midwinter. Plenty to do at home, child, I can tell you that.'

'Plenty,' said the girl who was not *krenn* any more, and she smiled.

Postscript

This is a story of two worlds, an old and a new, rubbing uncomfortably up against each other.

It is set around five thousand years ago in the south and west of the country we now call England. This was long, long before any 'English' people had got up out of their muddy homes in mainland Europe and sailed across the sea and up the rivers to settle here, before Julius Caesar and his Romans invaded, and even before the people before them.

It is an invented story, of course, but all the detail about how people lived is as accurate as I can get it. Here I have to thank Aubrey Burl, who very kindly read an early version of the story for me and saved me from some horrendous mistakes. I knew there were no rabbits here then, but I did not know about the horses. There may have been some around but no one was riding them yet, even the grandest people travelled on their own feet. I did not even realise that the huge stone mauls, used to shape the standing stones, were not made of granite but of sandstone. For all Dr Burl's careful corrections and his generous encouragement I am more grateful than I can say.

In the story Krenn finds she has to travel between these two worlds, and it is not easy. She starts at what is now Withypool on Exmoor and goes from there along the Brendon Hills, the Quantocks and the Somerset Levels. She splashes across the Levels, much wetter then than they are now, to Glastonbury, where the red brook still runs, then to Stonehenge, and after that to Avebury. Where she goes next is up to her.

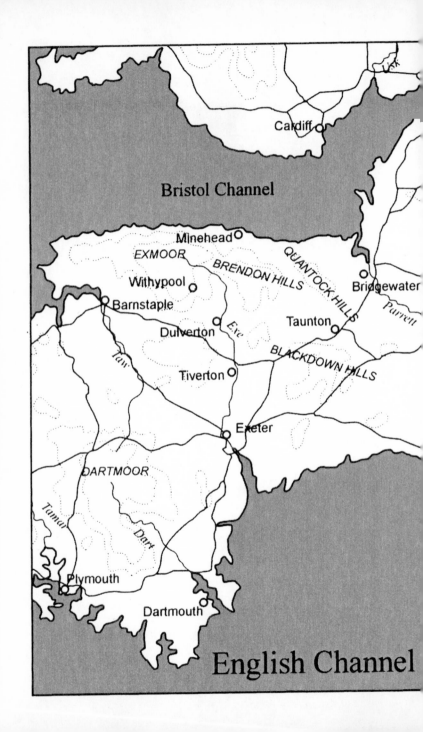